DREAM
UPON A STAR

DREAM
UPON A STAR

VOLUME ONE: THE BOY IN BLUE

YUMA

Copyright © 2023 by YUMA.

Library of Congress Control Number:		2023915197
ISBN:	Hardcover	979-8-3694-0545-1
	Softcover	979-8-3694-0544-4
	eBook	979-8-3694-0546-8

All rights reserved. No part of this book may be reproduced or transmitted in any form or by any means, electronic or mechanical, including photocopying, recording, or by any information storage and retrieval system, without permission in writing from the copyright owner.

This is a work of fiction. Names, characters, places and incidents either are the product of the author's imagination or are used fictitiously, and any resemblance to any actual persons, living or dead, events, or locales is entirely coincidental.

Any people depicted in stock imagery provided by Getty Images are models, and such images are being used for illustrative purposes only.
Certain stock imagery © Getty Images.

Print information available on the last page.

Rev. date: 08/14/2023

To order additional copies of this book, contact:
Xlibris
844-714-8691
www.Xlibris.com
Orders@Xlibris.com
852540

CONTENTS

VOLUME 1: THE BOY IN BLUE

Prologue 1

Chapter 1   A Goblin Mess...5
Chapter 2   The Boy in Blue...25
Chapter 3   Odd Encounters 49
Chapter 4   Siege on Alpherg Palace 75
Chapter 5   Tyrant King Gibbous 107

Epilogue 125
About the Author...131

*To Samantha, without you I would have
never been able to write this.*

VOLUME ONE

The Boy in Blue

Star light, star bright,
The first star I see tonight.
I wish I may, I wish I might,
Have the wish I wish tonight.

Starry eyes, full of life,
Look up through the darkened night.
I hope and pray, I hope I may,
Have the power to grant your wish tonight.

PROLOGUE

The country of Sol is an island nation that exists in Kanosei, the World of Possibility. It is said that Sol was one of the first places to be created in the material world after the great battle between the Nashi and the Sozo, and often is regarded as the Land of the Sun. Many people find different reasons to venture to the island—starting a new life, retiring and enjoying what's left of one, or even going on a grand adventure beyond the wildest of imaginations. Upon the ship *Voyager* sailing to the main island, one such group has found itself in hopes of such said adventure.

A young satyr, by the name Dawn Kernunnos, is sitting on top of a barrel, stringing her fiddle. Her emerald eyes gleaming in the sunlight, and her bronze skin absorbing it. Her feet are bare, revealing her bovine hooves and goat-like lower half. A light-colored, loose-fitting tunic covers the upper part of her body, with a leather belt at her midsection, with a rapier holstered at her side. Beside the barrel is her brown bag full of all her belongings that she had packed from the Fey Realm where she calls home.

She looks up for a moment and catches the eyes of a small group of children looking at the curled horns jutting out of her jet-black curly hair. She smiles and sticks out her hand, showing them that it is empty, and then twirls it, making a bow appear seemingly out of nowhere. Proceeding to close her eyes and click her hooves together, she begins to play a soft yet upbeat melody on her instrument that the young ones enjoy.

Near the edge of the ship, two individuals watch the water break against the starboard side of the vessel. One, a changeling in mud brown leather armor by the name Zua Apis, is morphing her face to better suit herself in the upcoming new environment. Long brown hair and a more human complexion over her usual pale skin, full black eyes, and silvery tangled hair.

Her armor is stained with small splotches of dried blood and adorned with many cuts all over, probably from all her battles. On her back is a bag like Dawn's, and at her waist is a single dagger glinting in the sunlight and a short sword sheathed in leather. Her black leather boots are worn and seem as if she has grown in them her whole life; but as she completes her transformation, she looks like a normal adventuring human woman. She turns to the person standing next to her, stretching her arms out as if proud of her fresh appearance and looking to be praised.

"What do you think, Urania?"

The taller woman standing beside her brushes her raven black bangs out of her face, revealing her curled horns and blue-toned face. Her demonic features extend to sharp fingers and a spaded tail poking out of her black leather armor with a dark cloak hanging over her shoulders, covering a dark bag and a satchel hanging at her waist. The hood of her cloak is down, allowing her to see the full scale of her friend's metamorphosis.

Her name is Urania Radium, and she is what is known as a half-demon, born from the taboo relations of a demon and a human. She smiles softly and laughs a bit, showing off her fangs, while placing a hand on her friend's shoulder.

"You look great, but I do miss your *real* face, Zua."

The satyr's song comes to an end, and she realizes that a larger crowd has flocked around her like moths to a flame. They cheer and applaud her for an exquisite performance as she climbs on top of the barrel she was sitting on and bows multiple times in every direction. Dawn returns to the floor of the deck and walks to meet with her other two companions, smiling and waving to people she passes by along the way. This is the group which our story follows, and whose legend you will soon learn of.

Each of these individuals has received a curious letter from a mysterious person calling himself "The Boy in Blue"; however, none of them could recall who the sender was or who has ever addressed themself by such a moniker. And even further, the letter was even more cryptic, reading as follows:

I hope you receive this summons in good health. I must ask that you come to the country of Sol to aid me in a mission of dire urgency that will surely be recorded in history. Along with the letter you are currently reading, I have gifted you tickets aboard the next ship to Sol, *Voyager*. Please do join me and you will be rewarded with the greatest item in all of existence after we are done. Meet me in the Central Plaza in Alpherg.

—The Boy in Blue

CHAPTER 1

A Goblin Mess

The midday sun shines down as the ship drifts slowly into port and sailors tie the boat to the dock, drop the anchor, and begin hustling about their work. Our group finds that they have arrived in the port city of Alpherg, filled with harbor smells of the salty misty ocean breezes mixed with market fish, which hang on lines in vendor stalls all in rows along the walkway. Not only do the sailors begin to move about their business, but so do the travelers, migrating into the streets and venturing to the tents set up to buy fresh merchandise.

The trio of girls steps off the wooden plank extending from the ship, allowing passengers to exit onto the docks of the harbor itself. White concrete blocks arranged in a neat fashion make a path leading all the way to the city limits. Dawn leads ahead of the other two, turning to face them with excitement painted all over her bright face. Grinning from ear to ear and puffy, rosy cheeks, she clicks her hooves on the pavement and gestures to the city.

"We made it! I wonder what kinds of amazing things we'll find here! I hope they have things that I could use for my craft."

Zua turns to Urania and cups her hand over her mouth so the bard wouldn't overhear her.

"Do you know if all fey are this weird in cities?"

Urania tosses her shoulders up and continues forward with Dawn, her tail swaying from side to side, brushing up against the stalls as they walk by. Ahead, she sees a man wearing a green tunic and a white bandana. A short bushy brown beard rests on his chin and he hangs up a number of salmon from the roof of his stall. As Urania approaches him, the man smiles gently, leaning up against the wooden countertop.

"Ah, fresh faces! What can I do for you? Got some fresh catches just this morning if you're looking to buy."

The demon girl looks up and down the wares lined up in front of her. The ceiling has fish hanging from their tails, while on the counter, the man has displayed small trinkets and salts of various shapes, colors, and sizes for viewing pleasure. Urania picks up one of the larger pink salt stones, lifting it toward the sun. She peers through it, inspecting how dense it is through its opaqueness with sunlight.

"Hey!" Zua's voice pipes in, gaining the attention of both her friend and the vendor. "Don't go trying to steal anything right off the ship, okay?"

"I was just looking! I'm not stealing anything . . . yet." Urania's face puffs up to a slightly red hue.

The man, not sure of what to do about the information he has just received after meeting the new customers, begins to pull some of his more expensive-looking products toward him with his arms. Urania places the salt back on the counter, smiles at the man, and then turns around and sighs.

"Come on, guys!" Dawn turns to face her companions as they continue walking toward the entrance of the city. Each step is followed by a small skip, accompanied by the sound of her hooves clicking on the stone.

"Let's try not to make any enemies on our first day here, all right?"

The other two take a glance at each other and raise an eyebrow, not sure if it was possible for them to not stir up some excitement. Unlike the bard, they were bounty hunters and already had a lot of enemies due to their pasts, not to mention they were also wanted in many countries by many people. Zua sighs as well, pulling out the letter she received from her pocket.

"Say, Urania, Dawn," she speaks up, reading the letter once more as they walk on, using her other hand to hold onto Urania's cloak so as not to bump into anything.

"Do you know *when* we're supposed to be meeting this 'Boy in Blue'?"

Urania's tail perks up for a moment and then slowly drops down to the ground, brushing against the street. Dawn closes her eyes proudly and points a finger to the sky, opening her mouth to speak but nothing comes out. Her finger falls as she slowly turns around with an embarrassed look on her face.

"Yeah, well, I have no idea."

The changeling and demon grimace at each other, while the satyr steps backward between them and wraps her arms around their shoulders. She squeezes them softly and grins optimistically. Zua catches her gaze and can't help giving her a slight smile.

"Don't worry," Dawn reassures them, "because I'm sure we could just ask around if we need to."

The group continues down the road, until they reach the limits of Alpherg. A large crowd seems to have gathered around a tall wooden archway greeting them into the city. Urania peeks her head up a little bit higher above the crowd, standing on her toes, assessing the situation to the best of her ability, when she spots something about ten feet in front of them.

A small child appears to be standing at the entrance, greeting people and attempting to hand them something from what appears to be a small woven basket. Her golden hair radiates like the sun, while her brown skirt waves with the motion of the crowd. Unable to get a closer look, Urania falls back on her heels and turns to the others.

"There's a lot of people trying to get in the city, but it looks like we'll be there soon."

A little time passes, and they make their way up the entrance. The large wooden plank above them has Lower Plaza painted in black with a yellow background and opens up into a large area with many different races and people crowding the streets. Dawn feels a slight tug at her shirt and looks down to see a little green child's hand connected to a little green goblin child.

Her hair is gold and curly, and her dress is brown and worn, with a few colorful patches here and there that appear to patch up holes or tears. Her big dark eyes seemingly grow larger as if pleading to the satyr for attention, while small drops of sweat line her forehead. Two tiny horns protrude from her locks and her ears droop from either side of her head. Dawn takes a moment to process and is overcome by the adorableness of the small girl.

"Maps!" the child says exhausted yet enthusiastically. "Please feel free! They are free after all."

At the sound of a tiny voice, the other two look down at the goblin child and feel a rush of adorableness flood over them. Dawn bends down to eye level and smiles gently to the girl. The child, taking a small step back but without any hesitation, continues to persist that they take her maps and holds out a brown parchment scroll with a red ribbon around it.

"Why, hello there, little one," Dawn's voice speaks loud enough to be heard over the crowd, but soft enough to not be shouting in the girl's face.

"What's your name?"

"Albedo."

Albedo begins to swing about, making her skirt twirl slightly. The young women feel their hearts being pierced by the sweet innocence of the youngling and let out an awe in unison.

"How old are you, Albedo?" Zua stands up a little taller, trying to impose some pride on the girl.

"And what are you doing out here too?" Urania leans over Dawn, cushioning herself in the satyr's hair while propping herself up on her horns. Albedo looks flustered for a moment and glances down but regains her composure and answers confidently.

"I'm seven today, and I'm working on giving maps to people while papa is out doing business."

"Seven today?" Zua repeats, thinking about what the girl meant.

"That means today is your birthday!" Dawn exclaims excitedly, clapping her hands together and resting her face on them. The young goblin nods stiffly yet proud, as if to impress the new visitors.

"Yes, I've been working very hard handing out maps, but I haven't given one out yet today."

"Well, we'll take three! How's that?" The demon sticks up three fingers for the goblin to see, and the young girl's eyes fill with joyful tears as she hurriedly pulls out three scrolls from a basket behind her.

The trio swoons over her again and happily takes the scrolls, placing them in their bags. They watch as the little goblin girl jumps around out of happiness as they decide to continue with their quest. Dawn gets off the ground and waves goodbye to their new friend.

"Thank you! I hope you enjoy your stay in Alpherg!" Albedo calls out to them before they are completely out of range to hear her.

"We will!" Urania calls out over her shoulder, waving goodbye to the goblin.

"And if you see my papa, tell him I was good and gave people three maps today!"

The young girl watches as the trio fades into the bustling crowd, waving farewell viciously, all while jumping and praising herself for her accomplishment. Our three adventurers, now in the Lower Plaza of Alpherg, stumble into the main hub and find that festivities are taking place a little way to the left of the city entrance.

Four small striped tents are set up on either side of the open space, each with games and activities to do. An older woman is sitting in a wooden chair under one of them, holding the palm of a young man, while children run around with streamers and sparklers in hand. Just behind the tents are several tables with people feasting and talking, with the largest wooden table holding a massive array of food, including a large roasted bird and three large barrels of ale. Looming over all of this is a gigantic spruce tree with streamers coming off the top, connected to children holding them at the ends on the ground, dancing in a circle around the behemoth plant.

"A festival!" Dawn springs up off the ground and clicks her hooves together. As she lands, she spins around and gestures to the others that they should investigate.

"Oh no, the bard's got that look in her eye again." Zua covers her face with her hand. Dawn grabs Zua and Urania by the arms and huddles them together.

"Listen! We don't know what time we're supposed to be meeting with this guy, right? So why not have a little fun in the meantime? What's the worst that can happen?"

"She's got a point." Urania looks over her shoulder, trying to eye anything that looks mildly entertaining to her. "Maybe we should learn a little bit about the culture while we're here."

"You know, for a thief, you have some odd respect for other races and their ways of life." Zua sulks for a moment but straightens up and nods her head at her friends' beamy eyed faces.

As Dawn gets a head start of the group, bounding over to the party scene, she notices something different. Maybe her eyes are deceiving her, but everyone at this gathering is a goblin like Albedo—green skin, droopy ears, and little nub-like horns. Zua and Urania reach her and come to notice the same thing. They aren't phased so much but get a sense of 'something else is going on here' from the situation.

The satyr makes her way over to look at a booth, during which the others head straight for the food. A young adult goblin wearing a red tunic and a pair of white trousers watches them approach, and a look of confusion strikes his face. He turns to his companions and sets his mug down on the table, gets up, and walks briskly over to them.

"Welcome! Are you two residents or just passing by?"

"We're just in the neighborhood and saw that there was an event taking place." Urania smiled, her fangs glinting in the sunlight.

"Are we intruding on something? We can leave." Zua gets a little antsy, not wanting to upset the goblins they just met.

"Oh, no!" The goblin waves his hands in front of him and laughs wholeheartedly. "We just don't get very many other people outside of us goblins coming to celebrate Aldebaran, that's all."

"Aldebaran?" Dawn asks, walking up with her face already painted and a streamer, a sparkler, and a mug of ale in her hands. Zua's eyes almost pop out of her head, surprised by how quickly the bard got around in a matter of seconds.

"It is our great goblin tradition where we celebrate our achievements for the month and get to sit back and enjoy the benefits of our hard labor. Today is the second day of the event, and tomorrow will be the last."

"I see," Urania thinks quietly to herself for a moment. "So it's a goblin tradition. That explains why there aren't any other races here and why you came to speak with us."

The young man smiles gently, yet nervously.

"Well, that is part of the reason, yes. We also don't seem to have a good standing in society anymore since King Ursa Major passed away six months ago. But please, stay as long as you like! Enjoy the festivities!"

He walks back to the table he was sitting at and starts talking with the other goblins there. Before long, a loud full belly laugh can be heard coming from the group as they clash their mugs together and take a big swig each.

"Well," Dawn's smile envelopes her whole face as she sets her things down and starts rummaging through her bag, "I think this calls for a little melody to spice up the joy!"

"You do that," Zua holds her head, walking away toward the food table. "I'm going to get something to eat. I'm starving."

"I'll come with you!" Urania tails her as the satyr pulls out a fiddle and bow, almost completely ignoring the fact that her friends left.

"Everyone!" she cries out over the crowd. Children stop running and all the adults fall silent. All their eyes start drifting over to the proud bard, raising her bow to the sky. She stands directly in the center of the tents and flashes a wink and smile.

"I would like to wish you all a fantastic Aldebaran!"

Dawn places the bow on the strings of the instrument and begins moving it in an aggressive yet light-hearted manner. Her melody picks up to a suitable tempo and wisps of magical dust start flying in the air around her, each of their own colors. Purples, greens, oranges, blues, and yellows sparkling and dancing around all the folks. Dawn stomps one of her hooves to get a constant beat going to keep time, which people begin to clap along with. Smiles and laughter break out as everyone continues their earlier activities, while others continue to dance along.

During the performance, Zua and Urania make their way to the large table with the food displayed on it. The changeling's eyes run up and down the spread, taking in as much as they could before deciding on what to get. She salivates at the sight of such a spectacular assortment of food. One thing she notices is the large roasted fowl in the center with small portions already cut out of it. She peers over her shoulder at the goblin they had spoken to before and calls out.

"Hey, this is really huge. What is it?"

"Why, that's the latest kill of our great leader, Oort." The goblin smirks proudly as he speaks. "I think it's the largest cockatrice he has found in Carina Forest this year. Those big birds aren't anything for our Oort."

"Where is this big guy then? I'd like to meet him." Zua smiles mischievously and puffs out her chest a bit.

Urania slaps her face with her palm and shakes her head, turning away and going back to the food to pick some out to eat.

"Afraid he's in the Central Plaza at the moment," one of the other goblins at the table joins in, being a little bit larger than the one Zua was speaking to and possibly a little older too. Instead of red, he is wearing yellow.

"His daughter has a birthday today and he wants to get her something he's had his eyes on for a while."

"Wait, does that mean?" Zua relaxes as she pieces together the information out loud.

"Ah, I get it," a muffled voice says next to the changeling. Zua looks up and sees her half-demon friend chewing a piece of meat while holding a fork with the source hanging off it.

"That makes Albedo Oort's daughter, right?"

"So you met little Albedo." The first goblin smiles again, this time softer and more welcoming. "Yeah, she's a cutie. Oort loves her to death and can't afford to see her sad."

"She's been working hard to save up money," the other says. "But even at one gold, no newcomers buy her maps. So she just started handing them out, but still, no one takes them. It's a shame. So Oort has gone into town in hopes of making it worth something."

The bard's music stops and a round of applause fills the plaza while Dawn takes multiple bows at the audience. Zua and Urania give each other a determined look and move toward the satyr's direction. During the show, Dawn had been bouncing from table to table grabbing small sips of ale that people had. Though she was of legal age to drink, she often found herself with a low tolerance for alcohol and getting very drunk very easily during her shows.

"Hey," she says, stumbling up to her companions, "th-there you guys are. Did ya hear my m-music?"

"Yes, good job," Urania said moving along, motioning Zua to grab Dawn. Doing so, Zua picks up the bard and throws her over her shoulder while goblins laugh and cheer. Dawn waves to everyone, hanging upside down as they head north towards the Central Plaza.

"Wh-where we going?" Dawn asks, very confused as to why they are leaving the party earlier than she wanted.

"Well, it's Albedo's birthday and she may want a gift," Urania said, walking past people in the busy streets of the Lower Plaza. "Her father is currently in the Central Plaza doing the same thing. Maybe we can meet him and help him find something for her."

"Wow!" Dawn hiccups, coming back to normal. Due to her satyr heritage, alcohol doesn't affect her the same as other races, and doesn't stay in her system for very long. She taps Zua on the back to let her down to which the changeling does.

"You guys learned a little bit already, huh?"

"Maybe." Zua looks around as they get closer to a similar looking archway to the one before, except this one is labeled Central Plaza.

"But we still haven't asked around about this guy who hired us yet."

"Oh, right," Urania hit herself in the face again, "we're on a mission, not a vacation."

"Well, let's ask around here then. This is where we're supposed to meet the guy."

Dawn smiles and skips along to the Central Plaza; her friends close behind.

Immediately, the group notices the sudden shift in atmosphere. The Lower Plaza seemed much more crowded and full of diversity, but the Central Plaza seemed scarce, with only elves, humans, and half-elves to be seen around. Even more, the joy and welcoming feeling is gone, being replaced by a feeling of tensity and dreariness.

"Weird," Dawn says under her breath. "It's like stepping into a new world in a new world."

"I'm getting a sense of some discrimination around here." Zua's eyes scan the area, counting the heads of the people and analyzing them like a wild animal sneaking up on its prey.

All the folks in this part of town look as though they are very well off, wearing gold trimmed silk clothes of reds, purples, and blues, all while walking around with their heads pointing to the ground. Some people catch a look at the trio and gasp and hurriedly go on with their business.

"I'm sure you're just exaggerating." Dawn laughs and walks up to the nearest person she finds. His nose is deep in a book, and his walking pace fast as he travels down the street.

"Excuse me. We're new here and were wondering if you could answer a question or two."

The man looks up and scowls at her. She can't tell if he didn't understand her or if his face always looks like that, but she smiles genuinely to mask her thoughts.

"I'm in a hurry!" the man snaps at her and, without another word, sticks his face back into his book and walks quickly away from her. He mutters fiercely to himself and Urania and Zua move so he can walk between them. After he leaves, they look over at the disheartened satyr who is now crouching on the ground and drawing in the dirt with her finger.

"How rude," she whimpers, making a sad face on the ground while the others snicker to themselves. Urania walks up to her and pats her head, reassuring her that everything will be fine. Dawn stands back up, but hangs her head low as they continue to search.

✦

"Halt! Stop the thief!"

A guard in a dark alley blows a silver whistle hanging around his neck and points ahead of him. His leather armor is covered with a few pieces of silver metal, with a bear crest inscribed on the center of his helmet. Four more similar looking men turn a corner about a hundred feet in front of him to see what's going on.

Two goblins are running toward them at a breakneck speed. The scrawnier, smaller one is shirtless and wearing baggy pants held up with a leather belt. His droopy ears flop about as he runs, and two nub-like horns poke out of his bald head. The other, at least five times his size, has a big black beard and large toned muscles dressed in scars and tattoos. His leather armor and horned helmet make him appear to be a marauder more than anything. The guards ahead of them form a wall with their bodies to try to prevent the suspects from going any further.

"Boss! More ahead!" The smaller goblin looks up at the bigger one, a little worried.

"I see 'em." The beefier goblin buckles down, sticking out his shoulder, and like a bull, picks up speed, ramming right into the barricade of men. "That ain't gonna stop me though."

"YO! Guard!" a loud and boisterous voice barks from a door next to the whistleblowing guard back in the alley. A scrawny wooden arm pops out as if it were asking for something.

The armored man looks over and down, his eyes cloudy with a pink misty haze. He reaches into his pocket and pulls out a small brown sack, dumping three gold coins into his hand. He extends his hand to the door, and the wooden appendage swipes the money. A brief grinding sound is heard and then a chuckle.

"Pleasure doing business with you!"

The two goblins continue running from the scene, now making their way into an alley leading to the Central Plaza's main gathering hub. The larger one looks over his shoulder to see that the five men are now pursuing them very closely. Whistles blowing and armor clanking, the guards scream at the two to stop.

"Dammit!"

The alley opens into the main square, and the bigger goblin starts rushing past civilians, each yelping and screaming. He stays with the smaller goblin, but slightly ahead by a couple yards, almost clearing a path for his shorter companion to easily make his way through the crowd. As they do, people begin whispering and sneering at them.

"Goblins? In the Central Plaza?"

"Should we stop them? Guards are after them!"

The thinner goblin scoffs and reaches into his pocket, pulling out a shabby slingshot. He bends over while still running and picks up a small grape-sized pebble and loads it into his weapon, turning back toward the guards while lining his shot. Just before he's able to fire it, he bumps into a half-demon girl and trips and falls to the ground, knocking her down too.

"Hey, you okay?" the girl's changeling companion asks, helping her up while guards catch up and tackle the now prone goblin. The larger, who is ahead by a little distance, stops and turns to face the group and soldiers; his hand reaching for his scimitar at his side.

"No, get out of here!" the little one yells out, as his hands are being bound with rope behind his back. "Albedo's waiting for you!"

Urania, the half-demon girl the smaller one bumped into, looks up toward the massive goblin in astonishment.

"But what're ya gonna do?" The green mass of muscle hesitates to step as the guards draw their weapons. They inch closer toward the bigger one and point their swords at him with a hand in a ready position.

"By order of the king," the one with the whistle and shiniest armor says, "I hereby place you under arrest for theft and trespassing in the Central Plaza." This one was obviously the leader of the group. Our adventurers, now caught in the middle of the event, look at both sides with anticipation.

"But we have permission to be here!" the smaller goblin breaks the silence. He squirms on the ground, tossing about while two other guards hold him down. A third gets on top of him and beats him on the head with the butt of his sword, making him pass out.

"Hey!" Dawn says, poking her head out from behind Zua and Urania, "That's enough! Don't you think you're being a little much!"

The men say nothing as the three stand up off of the unconscious body. The head of the group turns to her, and his hazy eyes meet hers.

"This doesn't concern you. Stand down, citizen."

"Citizen?" Dawn mumbles under her breath, raking her mind about where she's seen the haze around the man's eyes before.

"We're actually new here. But I think there may be a misunderstanding," Zua said, stepping between the guards and the bulky goblin. She looks over her shoulder and smiles at him. The goblin looks down at her confused, not knowing who she was or what she intended to do.

"If you continue to interfere, you'll be placed under arrest as well." The guards took a deep stance, readying themselves for a fight. "This is your final warning."

"Are you Oort?" Urania walked up the large goblin, admiring his tattoos. He nods his head as if to say "Yes I am" but tilts it to the side as if to show more confusion as to how she knows him.

"Who're you supposed ta be?" Oort looked down at the trio before him but was met with friendly smiles of relief.

"Just some new friends of your daughter, sir," Dawn says as she draws the rapier strapped on from her back. "I didn't have time to sharpen this back when we were on the ship, but I'm glad I still had it ready."

"Your daughter, Albedo, has a message we were to deliver." Zua pulls a dagger out of her belt and tosses it into the air. It spins around, and she grabs it dramatically and swings it to the side.

"She gave us three maps today. She's working very hard to make you proud." Uraina reaches into her cloak and pulls out her own set of daggers, holding the blades in a downward position.

"Men!" the leader guard shouts out and raises his sword toward the group of rebels standing before him. "Get ready to attack! Arrest them all!"

"I don't know who ya are," Oort smiles proudly, "but ya got spunk to stand up to some pigs ya just met. Even to help out an ol' man like me. I shall join ya in this fight, if ya don't mind."

One of the guards lunges toward the changeling, brandishing his sword and swinging it down at full force, but the girl is too fast for him and manages to dodge out of the way—not before giving him a quick humbling lesson with her dagger.

With a quick spin, she stabs him in his side and immediately pulls the blade out again, dragging a small stream of blood with it. The man yelps and grabs at his wound, crippling over slightly but still standing.

Dawn rushes over to a fountain a few feet away from the group with one of the guards following her. She stops and stares at it for a moment, taking in the oddity that it was. On top of a pedestal, a statue of a large man with a stomach twice his size, dressed only in undergarments, a cape, and wearing a large crown on his head can be seen holding his groin and urinating into the basin below. She let out a disgusted sound and hops on the ledge of the fountain. She gains her balance and whips her rapier out at the guard approaching her and parries his attack.

Urania, swiftly and gracefully, runs in the opposite direction, where a coach is parked and waiting for its riders to return. Similarly with her satyr friend, she hears the guard following her, and responds by leaping and climbing up the cart with ease. The guard stops, bewildered by what he witnessed, and the half-demon eyes her mark. She twists her foot on the roof to the coach and pushes off it, turning toward the guard below.

With a quick, deep, silent breath, she flings her dagger directly at him and pierces him directly in his chest, pushing him to the ground. As she lands over him now, she takes her second blade and stabs him again, pressing her blade into his heart until he doesn't move.

Oort draws his scimitar hanging from his side and lets out a large growl toward the two guards facing him. He looks down at the ground to see his companion lying face down and unconscious, but for a moment, all he can see is Albedo in his place. The guards rush at him, screaming and raising their swords to the sky for a preemptive attack. As the goblin snaps back to reality, he returns the guards advance with a full-bellied war cry and two powerful strikes, slashing both men across their torsos.

"Ya will not fell me today, ya scum of the earth!" Oort bellows as one of his attackers falls over, the other swaying back and forth but staying up right.

Zua, noticing that Oort is still nearby, steps back so the goblin is directly behind her. Oort looks over his shoulder and watches as the changeling focuses for a brief moment, shifting her form to match his own. Zua peeks over her shoulder to catch him staring at an almost identical copy of himself.

"HAHA! Lookin' pretty good there, youngin'!" The goblin and now goblin changeling draw their weapons back in front of them, one foe a piece, and charge directly into the enemies' range.

Dawn precariously balances her way around the narrow ledge of the fountain basin while the guard does the same chasing her.

"H-hey! Stop!" his calls fall on her with a timid expression. His foot slips, and he waves his arms around violently, trying to regain his equilibrium, while the satyr laughs at him and jumps down. As he finally finds his center again, he watches the girl kick up dust from under her hoof, pointing her horns at him like a bull readying to charge.

"Sorry about this," Dawn smiles, "but you asked for this." She lunges at the man, ramming her curled horns into his stomach and flinging him into the water. For a brief moment, as the back of his head smacks into the pedestal, she sees the haze around the guard's eyes dissolve, shattering almost as if it were like glass.

Urania pulls her dagger out of the corpse of the guard and looks around, seeing people terrified at the sight they just witnessed.

This isn't going to be good.

As she lifts herself up, assessing the situation with her companions and their new goblin friend, her attention is drawn to the alley behind her. A soft chuckle of a child almost rings in her ears. She jolts around, bringing her weapons up to guard her face and lowering her body. She steps slightly closer to where she heard the sound but finds nothing but a few barrels and crates in the darkness.

Zua charges toward the stumbling guard with his sword in a defensive position directly down the center line of his body. She lowers herself and drags the dagger in her hand up the blade of the guard, rising quickly and turning. By the time she stands upright again, her blade has knocked the guard's out of the way of his face, leaving him open to her fist, which was preparing for a full blown hook to the jaw.

With a cracking sound, she collides her attack with his skull and slams him into the ground with all her force. The guard coughs up a bit of blood as his eyes roll back and his body goes limp.

"Hell yeah!" Zua screams to the sky, raising her fist and weapon up in unison, celebrating her victory as any barbarian would.

"I like ya, shifter!" Oort laughs again, spinning around in an almost complete circle, dodging the slash of the man attacking him.

Oort counter attacks as he returns to face the guard, swinging his scimitar down on his opponent's arm and finishing his assault with a punch of his own. The soldier grabs at his arm for a moment, lowering his guard and screaming in pain. Within a second, he becomes silent, as the large goblin strikes him under his jaw, sending him flying backwards onto the ground.

As the final guard falls, Oort wipes his blade on his shoulder, cleaning the unwanted blood off. Afterward, he puts his weapon back in its sheath and races to his companion, shaking him softly. The goblin slowly comes out of his state of unconsciousness, but still dazed, looks around frantically for the guards that were chasing them.

"Boss," the smaller green creature speaks softly, seeing the three adventurers standing over the bodies of the incapacitated authorities, "what happened? Are you alright?"

"I should be askin' ya that." Oort, smiling out of relief, pulls the other goblin in close to him and squeezes tightly. Not too tight where the little one can't breathe, but enough where he won't be able to get out of his leader's grasp so easily.

Urania, with a confused expression on her face and still staring at the alley where she heard a childish laugh, walks briskly over to Zua who currently is shifting back into a more human-like appearance.

"I think we should do something about these guards so people don't get too suspicious."

"Yeah?" The changeling gave the demon girl a glare of almost pure disappointment. "That's definitely going to make the people who watched us totally off these guys forget about everything. Why not just throw them in the fountain if we're trying to not make a scene."

"Brilliant!" Dawn's high-pitched cheer comes from over in the fountain's direction. Urania nods viciously to agree that the idea is indeed a good one, all the while Zua sighs in disbelief.

The group, along with Oort, drag the bodies to the fount and dunk them into the shallow water. The water wasn't deep enough to swim in, but high enough that you could be submerged completely if you tried. The limp bodies, however, float lifelessly and seep blood into what was pristine clear water. Some of the guards are put face down, but no air bubbles rise to the surface to signify they were alive.

A passerby takes a glance inside the fountain, but reels back at the sight and he looks to the group as if asking for explanation. Dawn waves at him, smiling warmly, but the man sees it more of a threatening facade and scurries off in the other direction. Dawn droops down, again sad that people are not friendly to her attempts of welcome, feeling a large pressure on her back. She looks up to see the large goblin smiling happily at her.

"Ya three are incredible. As a token of our gratitude, we, the Alpherg Clan, are forever in ya'r debt." Oort bows his head out of respect to the group and grabs the head of the smaller goblin and forces him to bow in a similar fashion.

"No need to be so formal," Dawn waves her hands in front of her, a little embarrassed, "We just wanted to help, that's all."

Zua nods her head to agree and turns to face Urania, but notices that she has snuck away from her position next to her. Instead, the girl had snuck into the fountain and was looting the head guard, searching his pockets for any valuable items that they might miss if she didn't. She pulls out a small vial of red liquid and two gold coins.

"Cheapskate." Urania frowns and puts the gold in a small satchel hanging off her waist and the vial in her backpack.

She feels the gaze of someone and turns to Zua's direction and giggles softly. The demon climbs out of the water and joins the shapeshifter again, feeling as though she won't find more even if she tries.

"Why did these guys attack you anyway?" Dawn asks Oort.

The two goblins lift their heads up, turn to face each other, and then the group again. Oort turns slightly and pulls from his pocket a small doll with blonde curls and black button eyes sown onto it.

"Ya said ya met Albedo, my daughter." The goblin sounds slightly embarrassed but raises the toy up proudly for all to see. "It be her birthday today, but I hadn't gotten her a gift yet."

"Albedo has been trying to save up for this here doll," the other goblin says, his ears dropping to the sides of his face. "I told the boss about it, and we decided to get it for her instead."

"That's so sweet," Urania swoons for a bit. Zua's eyes narrow and she places a fist under her chin as she thinks out loud.

"It's her birthday, you wanna get her something, and you did. That still doesn't explain why you were chased."

Oort's eyes shift around, looking at the people in the plaza. All of them were looking at the group, some covering their faces, others cupping their mouths and whispering to each other.

"Ya see," Oort now lowers his head to the ground and begins to stroke his beard, "the Central Plaza is restricted to goblins by the order of King Gibbous."

"Restricted?" Dawn gasps.

"King Gibbous?" Zua asks.

"But why? That's not fair," Urania chimes in. The smaller goblin waves the trio to huddle in closer to them so they can speak more quietly. He points to the statue on top of the fountain, still relieving itself on the guards below.

"You see, King Gibbous came into power about six months ago and banished goblins after an incident. The guy's got a really bad temper and is easily put into bad moods."

"He's made it so that we goblins can't even step foot in the Central Plaza without permission," Oort grumbles to himself, stomping his foot and creating a small crater on impact.

"So why don't you just get permission instead of sneaking in?" Zua replies. "That seems like the most logical thing to me."

"You see we *do* have permission." The smaller goblin pulls out a form from his pocket. The document is a simple slip giving Oort and one person, of his choice, to enter the Central Plaza on this exact day.

"But the guards ignored that anyway and attacked you?" Urania scratches one of her horns out of confusion while the green creatures nod in unison.

"Ya see," Oort put the doll back into his pocket, "we visited this place called Mishaps and Misfortunes. Only place in town that sells items like this. However—"

"The shopkeeper, Dobs, isn't always known for getting his items legally." The scrawny goblin clenches his fists tightly and grimaces. "We probably fell into a trap anyway set up by Dobs and the guards to capture the boss here."

"Enougha that!" Oort booms and places a hand on top of his friend's head. "We ain't got proof of anythin' and I don't fear the likes of Dobs."

"Maybe we could investigate this for you?" Dawn looks to her companions for support. As the others trade a glance they turn to the satyr and nod in agreement.

"That's kind of ya, but we'll be fine." Oort laughs and smacks his bulging belly. "We best be goin' though. Albedo must be waitin', and I need some of that bird in my belly!"

The trio moves aside to let the goblins through as they make their way back toward the Lower Plaza. The smaller one stops briefly and looks over his shoulder at the girls before running back to them.

"Let me mark on your map where his shop is."

Dawn pulls out her map and the goblin takes out a pencil from his pocket, placing a small X to the far lower right part of the Central Plaza. He smiles, recognizing Albedo's crude drawings of the city, and hands it back.

"Be careful if you go there. Keep your wits about you." He turns to leave, taking a step forward. "And thank you for saving us."

Dawn feels a small amount of joy fill her chest as she watches the goblin catch back up with his leader. The two walk into the Lower Plaza and disappear into a crowd of people.

Mom. Dad. We just got here, and I already am making my own story and friends.

"Well," Zua places her hands on her hips, looking around at the chaos they created, "I say we go check this place out."

"Agreed." Urania's face turns to a serious scowl, her eyes piercing the statue of the half-naked king. "If there's a chance that Albedo could be in danger, we need to investigate."

"Also," Dawn lifts a finger in the air, "if this shop is the only place to find gift like items for a child, we can get her a birthday present there too."

"Marvelous! Superb! Absolutely breathtaking!"

The trio stops their conversation short, each turning around and drawing their weapons once more. Their backs pressed up against each other, they scan the area from all angles.

Urania is the first to notice that a young boy is standing in the sunlight on top of the wagon carriage by the alleyway she heard sounds coming from. He is dressed in all blue and smiling from ear to ear.

CHAPTER 2

The Boy in Blue

On the roof of the carriage is a young looking boy with snow white hair cut short. His eyes are a pale blue, twinkling like a star in the night sky. His clothes seem lavish, being made of blues of all shades. A short-tailed coat with white dress shirt cover his torso, while darker navy pants and blue leather boots adorn his lower half. In his hand is a small golden disk shaped object, no bigger than his palm. He presses a button on the top of the disk, opening it and revealing it to be a pocket watch. After a brief gaze at it, he closes the watch, places it in his coat pocket, and smiles down on the group.

"Hey," Dawn elbows Zua in the side, "do you think that's our guy?"

"So, it was you I heard?" Urania points a blue finger in the direction of the child, who continues to smile and even lets out a small chuckle.

"Guess you're a little more perceptive than I thought. But not that good." The boy jumps down from his perch and lands on his feet so gracefully that the girls lower their guard and weapons. Zua, being the first to snap out of the awed state, points her dagger up to the boy.

"Who are you? Tell us your name."

"Comet. Comet—" The boy thinks for a brief moment and then grins like a cheshire again. "Yeah, just Comet."

"Your parents must have hated you if they named you that." Urania looks down at the child and notices that he's completely relaxed and gets a sudden shutter.

"Haha! That's funny!" Comet bursts into a short laughing fit, flicking a tear from his eye. "So, how was the trip? Everything go okay?"

25

"Yeah," Dawn tilts her head side to side, a little confused as to what she was expecting their hirer to be. He did sign the letter as "The Boy in Blue" but she didn't think it would be so literal.

"Awesome!" Comet's grin returns, beaming his teeth for almost the whole world to see. "Also, I see you got to meet the locals. The goblin clan are friends of mine. But I witnessed your little spectacle too."

Comet points toward the fountain, and Zua looks over her shoulder at the bodies they piled into the water. It was completely crimson with the watered down blood now mixed into it. People had actively avoided it before, but now it seems like no one was even coming close to it. The barbarian turns her head back to face the child, but to her surprise, he is gone.

"Your skills are impressive, but execution is a little less than desirable," Comet's voice comes from behind the group, and each of the girls turn in shock to face the blue boy now standing behind them facing the fount.

"How'd you do that?" Urania gasps. Comet says nothing but instead takes out his pocket watch and looks at it again for a moment, out of sight of the others. The girls move in a little closer to see what he is hiding from them, and at that moment, the boy's whole body begins to quiver. They all lurch back and ready themselves for whatever is coming next.

"Woohoo! That's definitely something I gotta try for myself!" Comet turns to face them once more, now eyes beaming with delight and joy, though his face was quite a frightening sight to see right away. He raises his hand, one still with the pocket watch in it, up to his face and squirms around.

"What?" Zua asks nervously, getting a little frustrated at the mystery surrounding their encounter. "What do you mean? What's going on? Answer us!"

"Right, right." Comet gestures with his hands for everyone to relax and starts pacing slowly in front of them. "You guys are strong, way stronger than I thought. So I wanna test that strength. What do you say? Got some energy to spare on little old me?"

"Fight the guy that hired us?" Dawn tilts her head in confusion again and looks over to Urania for help. The demon gulps loudly and nervously tries to find words.

"You want us to fight you? Why? That just doesn't make sense to us."

"Oh, no, no, no, no!" Comet raises hands in front of him and shakes them out of disagreement. "We're not fighting. More like playing a game. Yeah! A game! I love games!"

Zua scowls at the child and growls to herself.

Is he serious? Is this really the guy we're supposed to be helping?

"Fine!" Zua stomps her foot forward and crosses her arms over her chest, puffing up a bit to make herself bigger. "What's this game then, *Comet*?" Even with a slight bit of attitude in her voice, Comet laughs and taps his feet on the ground out of excitement.

"Three minutes." As the child sticks out three of his fingers and grins menacingly. "If you can land a hit on me in three minutes, you win."

A unison wave of shock hits the group, and a looming sense of fear follows. They look on at the boy, still holding his hand up, and wonder what he had in store for them. First off, he would be outnumbered three to one. Second, they had combat skills and were much older than he was.

"Are you sure that's fair?" Urania takes a small step back, feeling a sense of danger coming from the kid. He smiles genuinely and innocently at her, nodding once with a hum of confirmation.

"What do we win when we do land a hit?" Zua asks, even more annoyed now. Comet thinks for another moment and looks down at his pocket watch resting in his hand.

"If you win," he lifts his face up smiling once more, "I'll tell you something secret. Fair?"

"Better than nothing." Dawn draws out her rapier and assumes a ready position.

Comet dances on his toes out of excitement once more and squeals with delight.

"This'll be so much fun! Come on, let's see what you got!"

With a multitude of spins and a flourish with his pocket watch, the boy raises the golden object up to his face for everyone to see, then places it behind his back. Zua, now completely annoyed by the waste of time, lunges at the child with great speed. Comet closes his eyes, tilts his head, and smiles. With no hesitation, the changeling pushes her dagger through the air between them directly at the boy's stomach.

"Zua Apis. Changeling," Comet says in a serious yet light-hearted tone. "You are the orphan child of a small village, correct?" Zua's eyes widen as the boy reveals his knowledge, but more so at the fact that just as she was going to contact him, his body glides out of the way.

"How do you know that?"

"Furthermore," Comet continues, now inches from the changeling's face, "you were raised in *that* orphanage, yeah? You didn't make very many friends but ended up getting adopted by an artificer. You left and joined him, honing your craft right? How intriguing!"

"Shut up! Who are you?" Zua angrily grabs her sword and draws it viciously at the boy's neck.

Comet, once again, deflects and leans backwards, the top of his head almost touching the ground. Zua, seeing the opening, redirects her blade and attempts to skewer the cocky child. She clangs as the tip reaches the ground and Comet is standing behind her, back to back, giggling to himself.

"You're very strong, and even have some skills in hunting and combat. But I think you got something on the inside that you've been neglecting."

Zua's eyes darken as she meets the confident gaze of the boy in blue peering down on her. His nose pointing to the air and mischievous grin painted on his face.

"What are you?" The changeling steps away slowly from him and notices that he has had his arms behind his back the whole time.

Impossible! He's too quick for a kid.

Comet shifts his menace toward Urania and flashes the whites of his eyes at her. She shivers and in an instant finds the boy up close to her next. He lifts his hand up and pokes at one of her horns, still holding the golden watch.

"Urania Radium. Half-demon. Also a bounty hunter."

The girl raises her arm up to push the boy away, but Comet hops backward about a foot and moves to the side. Urania stumbles, trying to keep her balance, and looks up to the child. He was looking down at the watch.

He might have info, but he's leaving himself wide open. Either he's overly confident, or we might have bitten off more than we can chew.

"Similarly, you were orphaned and were taken in by not just one hunter, but a whole clan! How exciting! A shame what happened though, but you're here now, so that's all that matters."

Urania swings her dagger back and forth with large motions, while Comet bobs and weaves out of the way perfectly while still maintaining focus on his watch. His eyes lift slowly for a second and say, "You know you can't hit me like that."

"How do you know this stuff?"

"I'd be a bad hirer if I didn't do my research." The boy's laughter brought down his serious attitude a moment before, and Urania can't help but think that he was actually not taking the exercise he insisted on seriously.

"However," Comet says, dodging a thrust of Dawn's rapier, "I can't help but wonder if you think that someone is still out there. I hope so at least."

"Stop being cryptic!" The satyr begins her advance with a few more thrusts, pushing the boy back toward Zua.

"Ah, yes! Dawn Kernunnos. The satyr bard." Comet grabs the tip of her blade between his finger and thumb of his open hand. "You come from quite the name in the Fey Realm. You even have a little bit of combat skill."

Dawn attempts to pull her sword back, but much to her surprise, it is completely immovable, as if it were encased in stone. She continues to try and pull it out from his grip while he monologues about what he knows about her.

"Your mother and father expect you to become great, but what is it that you want? I think you don't even fully know the extent of the possibilities open to you. Maybe we'll find something along our journey? But for now"—Comet clicks the button on his watch, and a blue light seeps out of the closed face. He releases his hold on the rapier, sending the satyr stumbling backward. She collects herself and looks up at him, preparing to charge in again, but is met with his index finger almost touching her nose.—"wanna hear a joke?" Comet's innocent smile covers his true intentions as he snaps his fingers in her face. "Laugh."

Immediately, tears form in the corners of Dawn's eyes, and the girl buckles down to the ground on her knees. Her cheeks puff up and her face grows bright red like an apple or molten hot piece of metal on a forge. Despite her resistances, the satyr's mouth bursts open, and a loud, full-body rampage of chuckles and snorts escape her.

Urania looks confused at her friend, who was now uncontrollably rolling in the dirt, laughing. She then turned her gaze to Comet's watch and then to Comet himself, who was peering directly at her. He crotches to the ground and springs into the air as Zua's blade passes by underneath him. Zua's expression of surprise is almost verbal while she watches her sneak attack fail. Comet descends down again, now placing one foot on the sword that was swinging under him, catching a short ride behind the changeling again.

When he arrives at his destination, Comet jumps off and opens his watch again. He lets out a small chuckle and closes it. But for the first time during the whole three minutes, he finally got to feel a sense of error as Urania was directly in front of him, reaching for his watch.

She moved so fast and so quietly! Shit! That was close!

The half-demon's gaze is wide and fixated on the golden object. Her fingers, for a split second, make contact with her target, and then the next are a whole foot away. Comet smiles warmly as she falls face first into the ground.

"Time's up! Nice try!" He snaps his fingers again, and the laughing bard slowly finds herself coming down from her fit. Comet tucks his watch back into his pocket and rests his hands behind his head.

"What'd you find so funny?" Zua turned to Dawn, not all too upset, but more confused.

"I-I-I don't know." Dawn's hiccups of small giggles impair her speech for a moment before subsiding. The girl sits on the ground bewildered at what she had just experienced.

"Whatever the case," Uraina lifts her face from the dirt, "I think we can say that this kid is our guy."

Comet bows humbly, as if to take the half-demon's words as a compliment. He raises himself back up and claps his hands together.

"Welcome to Alpherg, friends." The boy's greeting seems a little out of place to the trio, especially after he practically humiliated them not mere moments ago.

"Thanks, I guess." Zua helps both her friends onto their feet, and they dust off the dirt on their clothes and armor. "So, I guess we won't be getting any answers as to who you are or what you want us to do."

Comet laughs and pulls out a small brush from his pocket. He lifts it up to the sky and mutters softly to himself before stepping forward and grabbing Urania's hand.

"At least not today. My original plan was to get going right away, but Alpherg seems to be in a little bit of chaos." He moves the bristles on the backside of her hand in a star shape and then turns to Zua to do the same.

"Yeah," Dawn frowns, "we noticed that the goblins seem to be hated around here. Why's that?"

"Good question," Comet finishes with the changeling and continues to the bard. "I wish I had an answer, but as far as I remember, six months ago, the people of Alpherg lived in harmony with the goblins. Something definitely changed since then."

As he finished the final stroke, the child put the brush back into his pocket and started pacing in a circle thinking to himself.

"At least answer this," Zua says, lifting the hand he "painted" on. No visible mark is left behind and not even any wetness can be seen. "Seems rather pointless what you just did, but I'm curious what it was."

"Magic of some sort, right?" Dawn raises her hand up and examines it. She, too, can't see the mark he had drawn but felt a small amount of energy coming off of her hand.

"Good job, Dawn," Comet replies, not breaking his stride or gaze on the ground. "I gave each of you a mark that will appear when you need it. It will show that you are in allegiance with me. I have many friends in Sol, so this should help you out more than ninety percent of the time."

Urania touches the back of her hand and squints to see if she could see anything, but to no avail. Comet turns back to the group and slams his fist down onto his palm.

"Okay, listen. Let's call it a day today, but I want you guys to start tomorrow with investigating what's going on with Alpherg and my goblin buddies. I've only been out of Sol for six months, so it shouldn't have gotten this bad."

"That's fair and all," Zua says, nodding in agreement, thinking about how she would like to help out Oort and Albedo again, "but we don't really have a place to stay. Got any recommendations?"

"Got a map?" Comet extends a hand, and Zua gives him her map. "I got a friend named Quasar, he runs an inn just west of here." Urania sighs deeply, yet quietly to herself.

Parents REALLY hate their kids in this country.

"I also have two other friends named Twilight and Sidereal who run a supply store and forge respectfully. They may be willing to help you, not to mention I asked them to do me a favor with my next batch of hired adventurers."

Comet circles three areas on the maps and labels them properly and puts little stars in the center of the circles. He returns the map to Zua and turns, pointing off into the distance.

"That alley there should lead you to Twilight's, and if you keep going west, you'll hit Sidereal and Quasar's. I'll meet you guys tomorrow. Right now, I need to talk to someone else and catch up on things."

Without another word, but a wave goodbye, Comet begins to walk toward the southeastern part of the Central Plaza, melding with the crowd and disappearing into an alley. The girls watch as he leaves them alone, and then turn to face each other.

"That was eventful." Zua slouches, dropping her shoulders very exhausted. "I say we hit up these three places and call it a day."

"Agreed." Urania nods and turns to Dawn, who is shaking her head.

"No. You mean four. We still have one other place we need to look into as well." She lifts up her map and points to the X made by the goblin that was with Oort. The other two nod, almost forgetting about the information they received about the odd shop out; Mishaps and Misfortunes.

✦

The group comes up to a dark alley with very little traffic, actually no traffic it seems at all. Some crates and barrels are lined up in a way that makes it difficult to walk, having the girls take an uneven path to the shop ahead of them. A large makeshift wooden sign lay propped up beside a sturdy door that reads Mishaps and Misfortunes in sloppy white paint. A small smiley face was etched into the o of Misfortunes, trying to give the eerie place a more pleasant appearance.

"You sure this is the right place, Dawn?" Zua grips her dagger, a little tense.

The windows are dark and seem to be covered in dust from the inside and outside. Cracks and holes are scattered along the glass while the wood seemed to be rotting. The roof has a few shingles missing and the whole place looks as though it has been abandoned for years.

"Yeah," the satyr showed the others her map that the goblin had marked. "This should be the place, but it looks like it's closed for today."

THE BOY IN BLUE

"Well, this might help us figure that out." Urania points down to her feet where another plank was. This one what longer and painted in the same white ink was CLOSED—Mind Your Own Fucking Business!

The group takes a closer look and realizes that underneath this plank is a whole pile of boards, broken into pieces that if arranged properly have the same message. Dawn sighs and turns to walk away, until she hears faint whispering from the others. She jolts around, wide eyed, and loudly whispers to them.

"No! We are *not* breaking into this place!"

"Hey, we didn't say we were breaking in," Zua whispered back, "only thinking about it. There's a difference."

"We just killed a handful of guards! I feel like one crime is good for one day," Dawn's hushed voice was followed by the sound of creaking. Both her and Zua shift their heads to Urania, who was now standing at the entrance of the shop, hand on the door knob, with the door wide open.

"Is it breaking in if it wasn't locked to begin with?"

As Urania and Zua waltz into the darkness, Dawn looks around to make sure no one is watching them. She lowers her head in shame and follows the other two, hating the methods they were abusing to see the shop.

The inside is strange, filled with large dark piles of junk reaching the ceiling. The air is musty and full of dust particles, it was even cold enough where they could see their own breath. Besides the piles of trash, only two things really stood out to them. The first being the most obvious thing, the ceiling.

Above them was what appeared to be a regular flat surface, painted in the most extravagant design possible, a vortex composed of purples and deep greens. But with the revelation that things were dropping from the vortex made it apparent that it was actually a portal! To where, they can't tell, but small objects fall from the center every few minutes.

The second was a large counter in the back of the room. Buried behind a few stacks of garbage was a small wooden table with a bell on it. Nothing was sitting on the table, but unlike most other things in the shop, it wasn't dusty at all.

"This place gives me the creeps," Zua says, but as Urania turns to comfort her, she finds the changeling rummaging through one of the smaller trash piles, pulling out a large egg shell and a wooden mask with big eyes and a smile.

"I don't think we should be in here," Dawn whimpers, holding herself shivering in the cold. "There's things falling from the ceiling, no one's here, and it's cold and spooky without a light."

"Then why don't you make one?" Urania asks. "There's magic for that right?"

"I don't know that kind of spell."

"Well, I guess we can leave." Zua takes the mask off her face and tosses it into a random pile of junk. "Doesn't look like we can buy anything while the owner is out anyway. What was his name again?"

"I think it was Dibs?" Urania scratches her chin, thinking back to the goblin's conversation.

"Dobs. It was Dobs." Dawn quickly rushes to the door. "And I agree. We've stayed long enough. The sun is setting soon. Let's see what Twilight's is like."

The other girls follow, but before leaving, Zua draws a smile in the dust of the window. Urania behind Zua closes the door the exact way she saw it when she opened it, hoping that would be enough to not raise suspicion of a break in. The girls leave the dark alley and go west toward their next destination.

The girls make their way down the narrow street of the Central Plaza, passing by some people they had seen earlier. Recognizing them from the commotion in the main area, the people quickly move past them, avoiding eye contact at all costs. Dawn continuously looks over her shoulder, sensing that someone is watching them after leaving the mysterious empty shop. Eventually, she bumps into Urania, who has stopped walking. As the satyr looks up, she realizes that they made it to their next destination: Twilight's Supplies.

The bell above the door rings as the first to enter is Urania again, and the first thing she notices stepping in is the woman sitting in the back of the store behind the counter. Her skin is of a deep blue tone, similar to the half-demon, except this woman had no horns and long, boney fingers. Her long silver hair is slightly neat and ordinary, but as it moves further from the head, the more tangled it seems. On top of her head is a large, black, wide-brimmed hat with a giant black feather sticking out of it.

As the woman sits, she threads a string and needle into a tapestry of some sort, the size being covered by the counter. The trio enters and begins to look around. The planks of wood making up the floor creak underneath them as they explore the items. Boots, robes, and even a small shelf of books; the store seems endless. Just as they would get close to a wall, it appears to stretch even further out from the center.

"Welcome," a very elegant and yet snooty voice rings in the air.

The group turns back in the direction of the counter to find the woman, still working on her project, but motioning them over with her long blue finger. As they reach the counter, Zua notices that the woman's nails are painted red and that she is wearing quite a bit of makeup, mostly making her lips larger and redder than any normal creature.

"My name is Twilight," the woman continues, still not looking up at the travelers. "And you are?"

"We're new here." Urania smiles and laughs a little bit. Twilight pulls her needle a little tighter than she had been, stops, and looks up slowly.

"You don't seem good at communication. I ask you who you are, and you reply with information I already know."

Twilight leans forward, and whatever she was sitting on groans as she does. Her eyes squint very narrowly, unamused by Urania's answer. Then a glint of light radiates from the girl's side, and the elderly looking woman's gaze is drawn to it. On each of the backsides of the group's hands is a star-shaped mark made up of a bluish-white light. Each of them notice after a second and look down and then back at Twilight.

"That explains it then," the woman returns to her original position. "Comet sent you. So, you're his new line of help, are you?"

"We are," Zua answers, nudging Urania with a smirk on her face. The demon sticks her tongue out quickly. Twilight looks down at Dawn and notices the satyr has her head down. She was bashfully twiddling her fingers and looking repeatedly at the small bookshelf.

"Comet did warn me he was going to send more people our way. He even said to make sure they stayed this time to discount all my wares for you."

Dawn looks up in surprise and the other two give the blue woman an equally shocked look.

"Something about making sure you're motivated. That boy is bad for business." Twilight turns to Dawn again and opens her mouth but is cut off by the sound of a bell ringing behind her.

The girls peer over Twilight's shoulder and notice a door with multiple bells with strings around it. One of them was ringing and shaking about. The woman sighs and turns around and moves over to the bell, pulling on the hanging string three times. Afterwards, she faces the girls again.

"Well, it was something meeting you all. If you need me, just ring the bell on the counter and I will be back as soon as I can."

Twilight opens the door, and the girls watch in awe. On the other side is a swirling vortex of greens and purples similar to that portal in Mishaps and Misfortunes. Twilight enters into it and closes the door behind her with a loud click. The sound of hooves clopping on wood follows. Zua watches as Dawn races to the bookshelf and starts skimming through bindings of the books on it. Then a shuffling sound, as Urania leaps over the countertop onto the shopkeeper's side.

"Hey!" Zua yelps. "What do you think you're doing?!"

"I just want to see what it is," Urania shrugs her shoulders in an annoyed fashion, creeping slowly to the door.

She places one of her ears up against it and listens carefully. In case Twilight came back, she didn't want to be on the wrong side of the counter. Slowly, the demon girl grabs the doorknob of the door and twists it slightly to see if it was locked. But it wasn't, meaning that she could attempt to open it. Carefully, Urania pulls the door open just enough for her to look through and peers inside.

"Well," Zua whispers, leaning up on the counter, "what do you see? Anything interesting?"

Urania gets up, and then yanks the door completely open, revealing a brick wall instead of the portal from before or even a space to walk into. She shuts the door gently and hops over to the other side again, stroking her chin in confusion.

"Dobs's place, and now this one too. What are these portal things?" Urania looks up and sees Dawn hunching over the bookshelf, muttering softly to herself.

"Damn," the bard exclaims, not finding anything that she wanted.

She was looking specifically for stories that were exclusive to Sol and its heritage. As a bard, it was common knowledge that you should know many different stories about the places you visit. However, all the books were stories that she already knew. As she is about to get up, she notices a small slip of paper wedged between two of the books.

"For more books, please consider visiting Bellatrix."

Stumbling on at least some small piece of something useful, Dawn stands up and makes her way to where the other two were. Zua is looking through various items, but putting each one back, while Urania was examining some of the robes, also putting them back after seeing the price tag.

"Well," Zua says, throwing a hat into a pile of other hats and headwear, "I can't find anything a kid would play with and I don't feel like waiting to ask her either."

"Agreed." Urania walks over, feeling beaten by the market for outerwear. "Let's try getting some answers about our mission at Sidereal's Forge?"

"That sounds like fun!" Dawn becomes excited, bouncing up and down like a child with candy. "I've never seen what a forge looks like in this realm, so I very much would like to see if they have rapiers."

"You really have a fondness for those sword twigs, don't you?" Zua chuckles softly. "But you know how to use them so I can't complain. Onward!"

✦

The girls leave the store and enter back onto the streets of Alpherg, walking further west. The sun sinking over the horizon, people start making their ways to their homes. The girls pass through the main area and see the large fountain again. With the bodies of the guards still in the water, Zua laughs to herself and her handiwork in the escapade from earlier in the day. For a first day in a new country, it sure was eventful.

They are a few blocks away from the forge, but they can still hear the faint sounds of a hammer hitting metal in the distance. As they arrive at their destination, the first thing they notice is that there was no door in the doorway. Instead, it is just a large brick opening with no security at all. Upon stepping inside the building though, the girls feel an overwhelming presence of heat from the fires contained by the furnaces and forge itself.

The sounds that they heard coming from the building grew louder, and the source was sitting on the other side of the room. A bald figure with a long twin braided beard in leather and cloth was working at an anvil. From behind he seemed like he was a human, but given his features, he was obviously a dwarf.

"Um, hello. Excuse me," Zua cups her mouth and calls out to the man. He looks over his shoulder, grunts, and continues to work.

"Well, that was rude," Dawn huffs, but immediately gets distracted by one of the walls. On each of them are a multitude of weapons hanging on display. Ranging from bows to swords, axes, and hammers, the forge is almost a complete arsenal for a small army. The satyr has never seen so many pieces of metal in her life, that she can't help gushing over everything.

"Hey, Sidereal, right?" Zua calls out, now a little more aggressive. "We want to talk to you."

THE BOY IN BLUE

The clanging stops. The dwarf turns to face the trio and snorts loudly, heaving himself over to a wooden countertop. As he approaches, Zua and Urania, the only ones paying attention to him, witness the dwarf grow in size. Bigger and bigger and bigger until he standing over them at almost a full ten feet tall.

"I am Sidereal," the dwarf's low voice shakes the ground. "What do you want?"

"Y-yeah," Uraina glares at Zua, "what was so important that we wanted that we had to bother this kind gentleman?"

"Um. I . . . uh," Zua struggles to find the words to communicate. With only a single thought in her head to not upset the giant dwarf any further, she looks down at her hand to see if the mark was glowing, and it is. She raises it and shows off the emblem.

"Damn that Comet," Sidereal sighs, rubbing his bald head with a table-sized hand. "He's bad for business, but I did promise him. What can I do for you then?"

"I have a few questions first," Urania pipes in, leaning in on the counter with her elbow.

"Are you buying something or just wasting time?" Sidereal points with his thumb at the item on his anvil. A large piece of metal is glowing red, but slowly is losing its heat and color.

"Oh, sorry," Urania says, now hitting her head slightly. "I just was curious if you knew anything about Comet or this mission we're on?"

Sidereal sighs again and looks down on the two disappointedly.

"I don't. Just that I'm supposed to discount items for your group. I don't work with him that closely. Talk to Quasar if you have questions like that."

The dwarf turns away and stomps back to his work, lifting his hammer and pounds on the metal before him. Zua looks to Urania only to find the half-demon pinching the bridge of her nose. She then looks around to find Dawn, who had discovered the rapiers not too long ago.

"Hey, Dawn!" the changeling calls out, scaring the satyr a bit. "We're leaving. We'll come back tomorrow or something. You can look at your fancy swords then."

"Rapiers!" Dawn exclaims and bounds towards the group as they exit. Sidereal's hammer stops for a moment as he looks over his shoulder at the group and then at the swords Dawn was looking at. With a simple head shake, he returns to his current project.

"A dead end," Urania grumbles to herself as the trio continues heading west. She was holding her tail now and pinching the tip of the spade between her fingers.

"Why are you so disappointed?" Zua asks, pulling out her sword and pointing it toward the sky. The last bit of sunlight reflects off of it until it completely disappears leaving the blade dark.

"Yeah, you weren't even looking for a weapon," Dawn decides to join in the conversation, getting in front of the two of them and walking backward to face them. "He makes armor and weapons and stuff, not answering questions of every person who walks in."

"I know," Urania puffs her cheeks, "but we're completely in the dark. Comet says he has a mission for us, but now that's on hold because Alpherg is in trouble? I thought the first one was important."

"Maybe it's related to the original mission?"

Zua's response is met with a death glare from the demon, making her shutter in her armor. Dawn giggles to herself, but then thinks for a moment.

"Actually, that doesn't sound far off. Maybe it is important to the mission. Of course, I don't know how it could be, but if you hire someone for something and then give them another task over the original, it has to have a connection, right?"

"Or he's just using us because he's lazy," Zua remarks, kicking a small pebble across the street.

"Yeah, we don't even know if we're getting paid!" Urania's realization makes her drop her tail and violently scratch at her scalp with her hands.

"Calm down. We'll get some answers from Quasar."

Dawn points to a large building with red roofing reaching up to the sky. They must have entered the residential district at some point because all buildings on the street seem to have a great number of stories. On this particular building was a wooden sign hanging off the horizontal metal pole, flapping in the breeze, with Quasar Inn—Best Rest in the Cosmos.

"That's oddly welcoming." Urania, seeming a bit more relieved, walks up to the door with her friends.

Inside, a tender, warm home feeling washes over the group. A flight of stairs stands directly ahead of them and to the left is an open area with tables and chairs set up all over. Three young and good-looking men in aprons are clearing off any leftover plates and food and bringing them to the kitchen located directly on the far side of the tavern space.

"Oh, welcome," a hushed, soft, gentle voice echoes from the right.

The girls turn in unison to find an elderly man in a lavish blue robe, laced with gold trim and designs sitting at a desk. His short white hair contrasts his long braided beard, which he is twirling between his fingers. A small pair of circular glasses rest on the tip of his nose, assisting him in reading a small brown book that he is holding.

"Can't say I've met you before. My name is Quasar. It is a pleasure." A gentle smile extends across his face as he leans forward to get closer to speak with them.

"Yes, hello." Dawn bows, waving her hand with flourish, attempting to be fancy. "We are new acquaintances of Comet, and he has recommended your lodging, good sir."

"I see." Quasar laughs softly, putting his book down on his desk. "I thought today was the day."

He waves his hand in the air, and a large tome floats off of a shelf from behind him. It carries itself all the way to the old man's hand, and he brings it in front of him, moving his hand over it while the pages turn on their own.

"Magic?" Zua asks the bard.

"Magic!" Dawn's eyes glow with wonder witnessing the spectacle in front of her.

"Ah, here we are!" Quasar points a finger on a page and moves it down slowly. "Dawn, Urania, and Zua, correct?"

"That's us." Urania nods, fidgeting as the elder turns to a drawer and takes out three keys. Each key looks similar except for one thing; each of the bows had a different number on them.

"Your rooms are paid for in full and are on the top floor, the seventh." Quasar hands all the keys to Zua, who distributes them out at random to the others.

"How long do we have these rooms?" Urania blurts out, ready to bombard the man with her unanswered questions. "A couple days? A week?"

"Oh my, heavens no." Quasar laughs again in a very friendly manner. He looks down at his ledger again and uses his finger to find the answer to her question. His face expresses a moment of unbelievable amazement but returns to a soft smile as he looks up to the group.

"Let's just say you won't be staying for that long."

"But how long? Will we have enough time to finish our job in Alpherg?" Urania's impatience is now written all over her face. Combined with worry and tiredness, the half-demon was on the verge of a mental breakdown.

"I don't think even your main task will keep you in Sol for five years." Quasar chuckles happily, closing the book and letting it fly back to the shelf.

"Five years?!" Dawn gasps.

"And the rooms are fully paid?!" Zua adds on.

"Not to mention," Quasar grins happily, "these are also our finest rooms, fetching our highest price. So you really got a deal."

"Highest price?!" Urania falls backward but is caught by a chair that magically scoots itself underneath her. Two more move toward Dawn and Zua.

"You will be using them for your entire journey in Sol, so make yourself at home." Quasar smiles gently again.

"So, our base of operations is here in Alpherg?" Zua looks puzzled. She knew Sol was a smaller continent, but she did not want to keep backtracking if they were halfway across the country.

THE BOY IN BLUE 43

"No, no." Quasar laughs. "You see my inn, Sidereal's forge, Twilight's shop, and a few other places have been given a strange and unique ability. They exist on rifts in dimensions that link the realms. We call these rifts Spatial Areas."

The girls look at him with confusion of what he was talking about.

"These places are able to link one place with another. So it may look like I have one inn, but instead, I own multiple, and they are all just threads from a center point in space-time allowing me to traverse between them freely. Same goes for the others. When you move to a new city, just request that we bring your items along there for you. No need to worry."

The old man is met with blank stares, and Zua squinting out of sheer disbelief. He nervously smiles, taking a deep breath in and out.

"You might have some other questions from today and about anything." The old man leans back into his chair again, waving his hand once more. A pipe hovers over to him and he places it into his mouth.

"I'll be happy to relieve you of any confusion now."

"I don't know where to start." Urania looks down at the ground a little overwhelmed.

"I do!" Dawn perks up and takes a seat in the chair for her. Zua follows her lead and sits down in her chair. "Who or what is Comet? He is not normal, that's for sure."

"Yes," Quasar puffs his pipe and smiles, amused by the bard's tone, "Comet is an exceptional boy. He's actually not from our realm. He comes from a place called Magnetar, the World of Wishes."

"Wait, so what does that make him? A god?" Zua crosses her arms and leans back in her chair.

"No, he's just a different kind of being. We call them Negai." Quasar blows a ring of smoke. "Or wish granters. They are born from the dreams of creatures in all other realms. They aren't normally found on Kanosei, but some find ways to do so."

"Okay, that doesn't explain why we had to play that stupid game." Urania frowns, looking away in embarrassment. "I think I know what makes him so slippery, but I couldn't grab his watch."

"Oh," Quasar's eyes light up, "so you almost got him, did you? In the sixty years that I've known him, I have never once thought of that. I could never match his speed nowadays."

"Wait, he's more than sixty years old?" Dawn exclaims. "He looks so young!"

"Negai age differently than most other races. They appear to be in their prime when they are actually considered old. A hundred of our years to them is just one." Quasar strokes his beard and thinks for a little bit. "I'd say he's about two thousand and seven hundred years old."

"Wow," Urania grabs her forehead and looks at the other two, who are just as mind blown by the information as she is, "that's a lot. So what about our mission?"

Quasar puffs on his pipe for a little bit, and the girls lean forward in anticipation. He closes his eyes and wrinkles his face as he tries to remember but opens them again with a somber look.

"Unfortunately, I don't really know myself. I do know he needs you to collect something since the other two adventurers he hired last time told me that. However, that is the extent of my knowledge."

"Wait," Zua rubs her chin while speaking, "you mean to tell us that there was another group before us?"

"Why, yes, of course."

"What happened to them?" Dawn nervously fidgets in her seat. One of her knees starts to bounce. She hadn't been outside of the Fey Realm very much, but the idea of a group before her failing, or even worse dying, was not comforting news to be given.

"Worry not." Quasar adjusts himself in his chair. "They were tasked with the same mission as you seem to be, but they fell short somewhere along the way six months ago."

"That's about the same time that the king died, right?" Urania ponders quietly.

"You don't think . . ." Zua darts a look from Urania back to Quasar, who shakes his head somberly. Dawn sits quietly, confused as to the correlation between the old king and the other hires.

"No, I don't imagine they are responsible for the late king's demise. However, there is a rumor, nearly confirmed, that they were seen with the Crown of Cepheus while heading toward the docks."

"Any idea where they were heading with it?" Dawn, trying to grasp what little understanding she could, pieces that the destination of the older group could be the resting place of the crown.

"As far as we know," Quasar strokes his beard, "they were said to have gone to Luna Island. However, in a few days they returned, the boat and crew a mess. Comet scolded them harshly and told them to leave Sol. That's when he left to find you three I presume."

The girls exchange a few glances among themselves, taking in the new information to memory. The events seemed to be lining up better now. First, Comet had hired a group of people to assist him in his mission, but then something happened when the king died and they took the crown, lost it, returned to Sol, and were exiled. Afterward, Comet left to find them, and then Gibbous took over as Alpherg's king. Right!

"What about Gibbous?" Zua stands up and clenches her fists. "I bet he took the throne right after the other king died, right?"

"Yes," Quasar nods, "but a little time went by. Oddly enough, not many people supported his idea of taking up the mantle of being king. But even though, the guards took him to the palace out of the blue just to officially crown him. Talk about from rags to riches."

"So, the guy wasn't even a noble or anything?" Urania looks down confused as Dawn stands up making her way to the stairs.

"I know we still have a lot of questions,"—the satyr yawns loudly—"but we should call it a night for now. Thank you for speaking with us, Mr. Quasar."

"Just Quasar is fine." The elderly man stands up and bows to the girls and the young men do the same thing. "We hope you rest well."

The trio heads toward the stairs, up to the highest level. Each of the levels was similar, having about six rooms on either side. But as they step up to the seventh, only four rooms are present. One is labeled as Head Manager, while the others have 7A, 7B, and 7C written on golden plates. The doors are simple, but the wood seems to be of a more expensive type, possibly mahogany.

The girls look at each other and then down at the keys they are holding. Without another word, they each move to the respective doors: Urania to 7A, Zua to 7B, and Dawn to 7C. Upon entering, they are immediately surprised by the state of their new living quarters.

Each of the rooms is furnished with lavish-looking beds fit for a noble or aristocrat. The sheets are laced with gold and made from silk. A large wooden wardrobe was on one of the sides of the massive bed, with a small, yet relatively larger than normal, nightstand. A brass lantern with a candle already burning sits up top of it with a small blue book with The Confraternity of Gemini in bright gold on the cover.

Zua, taking off her armor and placing it at her bedside, hops straight into the covers. Warmth envelopes her, but the silk keeps her body cool. Urania takes some time to flip through the book on the nightstand, and Dawn unpacks a few of her items and places her things around the room. Time passes for a bit, and eventually, the adventurers drift off into slumber, awaiting tomorrow's toils.

CHAPTER 3

Odd Encounters

The morning creeps in through the drawn curtains of Dawn's room. The bard pulls the soft cover over her head, groaning to herself, all while the light attempts to reach her eyes. It isn't that she didn't sleep well the night prior, just that she isn't the best with early morning rising. Next door, in Zua's room, she can hear movement. Her companion was probably waking up too and putting her armor back on, ready to start the day.

"Fine." Dawn throws the pillow from underneath her head to her side in frustration, forcefully lunging herself upright.

She shuffles out from under the silk layers of comfort to the cold wooden surface of the floor. Her hooves click as she walks to her things and dresses for the morning. She picks up her bag and sword and makes sure that they are tightly attached to her, but not too tight where she couldn't move. She steps toward the door and opens it to find Urania passing by to go downstairs.

"Morning," the half-demon girl yawns loudly as the both make their way to the descending staircase. As they continue to reach the lower levels, the sounds and smells of delicious food being cooked hits them, tempting them to pick up their pace.

As they reach the bottom, they are welcomed by a fuller-looking tavern scene than when they entered last night. Many different races are grouped around tables, eating their meals while talking and laughing with each other. Urania scans the room quickly and doesn't see anything that's too out of the ordinary in the public area. However, something peculiar was happening in the kitchen, which she could see thanks to the open viewing area past the counter where the waiters were grabbing plates to bring to tables.

A small boyish-looking figure with a blue bandana wrapping his hair is using a frying pan behind the counter. He is wearing a similarly colored apron over a nice white dress shirt with its sleeves rolled up to the elbows. The other cooks are applauding him as he flips a pancake and catches it back in the skillet.

"Is that?" Urania cuts herself off while tugging at the groggy bard, who had managed to doze off a bit while standing next to her.

"What! Oh, it's Comet." Dawn sleepily makes her way to the counter and lays her head down.

The boy notices the two hires and laughs, waving Urania over. When she gets within earshot, he pulls out a small pamphlet from his apron and hands it to Dawn and one to Urania, who leans up against the counter.

"Good morning, ladies!" Comet's face beams like a ray of sunshine. "What can we get for you today?"

"Are you playing chef?" Urania takes the menu and looks it over.

"Playing is such a mean way to think of it. I'm simply broadening my horizons!" Comet shows off his pearly white teeth in a flash. He leans up on the counter as well and looks over the crowd for a moment.

"I'll take some porridge," the blue girl responds to his food inquiry. "And one for the other two as well."

"Might I ask," Comet says, drawing his attention back to Urania, "where is your third head? You know, Zua." Urania looks over toward the stairs, expecting to see the changeling walking down on cue, but sadly is disappointed by no one at all.

"She'll be down soon. She takes her time in the morning, usually."

"Right. Well, three porridges is three gold in total." Comet sticks out his hand and Urania puts three gold pieces into it. The boy turns away and starts talking to the cooks and gets to work on the order.

A few footsteps approach the demon from behind, and as she turns to investigate, a hand pats her on the back. Zua then leans her back against the counter, with her elbows resting on it as well.

"Morning, Urania. Morning, Dawn." Her face was morphing again, as if she was practicing a new face that she had recently seen, but eventually brought it to the same one from the previous day.

"Comet's here," Dawn's voice, muffled by sleepiness and the wooden counter, pipes up for the first time since arriving down in the lobby.

"You don't say." Zua looks around trying to find him, then feels a tap on her shoulder. Urania motions to the kitchen and the barbarian's eyes almost pop out of her head seeing the boy in an apron.

"What the?"

"I know. Weird, isn't he?" Urania taps her fingers on the wood. "Bought us some breakfast, but now that you're here, I think we should ask him some questions when he comes back." Zua nods in agreement and looks back into the kitchen, carefully watching the mysterious child.

Comet, not having very much skill in cooking, more so watches the other cooks at their craft. He walks up to a few, asking them something, then receiving the item they are working on and attempting to make it himself. He does this a number of times, all the while Zua stares him down; her eyes becoming narrower with focus. After a little bit, he grabs three bowls and walks back over to the group.

"Ah, there's Zua!" Comet smiles again, placing a bowl in front of each of the adventurers. A small mound of sludgy oats fills the dishes and a wooden spoon sticks out from the side, inviting the girls to dig in. The aroma coming from the food is cinnamon with a hint of apple thanks to the three slices on the outer rim of the bowl.

"Food!" Dawn's head rockets up as a small groan comes from her gut. Comet giggles to himself as the group starts to eat.

"I bet you're curious about a lot"—the boy rests himself over the counter, propping his head up with his arm—"but we have some important business to address today."

"But you haven't explained the mission." Urania frowns.

"We asked Quasar about some things yesterday, but we're still lost," Zua joins in. "We need to collect something, and what's this about another group before us?"

ODD ENCOUNTERS   51

"Oh"—Dawn wipes her chin that has a little bit of porridge sliding down it—"and what's a Negai, and who is Gibbous?"

"All valid questions." Comet raises his hands, closing his eyes as if pained by the interrogating that was happening. He feels a bead of sweat on the side of his face and laughs timidly.

"Well?" the girls echo in unison, and the tavern falls quiet for a brief moment. Comet waves at everyone and they all resume their business.

"Look." He turns back to the girls. "I want to get you filled in, but we are a little short on time. We need to investigate what's going on with the goblins being ostracized, Gibbous being the new king, and why the guards are acting funny."

"Tell us more about Gibbous then." Urania sighs, settling for the little information they can gain.

"Well, for starters"—Comet tilts his head and looks up—"before I left to find you guys, Gibbous was a commoner who wasn't good with money. Whatever little he had or would obtain, he spent on alcohol and gambling. He has always been temperamental and would get into trouble a lot."

"Sounds like a bitch," Urania scowls at her porridge for a moment.

"He would harass women on the streets, and I was even called a few times to take care of him. He hates the goblins for some reason and even gets into fights he can't win with them. All in all, he's just an unfortunate guy."

"He *is* a bitch!" Urania exclaims, slamming her fist onto the countertop.

"Well, what do we do about it?" Dawn asks. "I'm sure that's where this is going since you told us a little bit about him."

"Hit the nail on the head." Comet snaps his fingers and winks at the trio. "You guys are going back to the goblin settlement in the Lower Plaza to gather some more intel on what happened during my six month hiatus period."

"Why us?" Zua groans. "Why not you? If it's anyone's fault that this didn't get prevented, it's yours!"

"I'm going to pretend I didn't hear that." Comet slumps a little bit, his face becoming very stoic. It was obvious though that Zua's words hurt. "I got something else I want to check."

He pulls out his watch and takes a deep breath. Urania's eyes glow, seeing the pocket watch once again. Comet clicks the button on top of it and the lid pops open. He peers at it for a good thirty seconds, closes it, and puts it back into his right pocket.

"I'll meet you guys down there as soon as I can." Comet hops over the counter, taking off his apron and bandana. He swings them over his shoulders, and they transform seamlessly into his blue tailed jacket.

"Find Oort and see what he knows."

Without another word, the boy makes his way to the entrance and leaves the tavern. Zua and Urania exchange a look, as though they could communicate telepathically.

Do we really have to go along with this? Zua's eyebrows rise up on her forehead.

Let's just go and see what we can find. Urania lowers her head to the ground and then lifts it back up to Zua with a look of determination. *We can't just leave Oort and Albedo in danger.*

Fine. You're right. Let's go.

"OH NO!" Dawn screams, breaking the silence of the group and creating one all around them. She begins to shovel down the food in front of her as if it was about to be taken away.

"What's with you?" Zua reprimands, feeling all the attention being drawn to them.

"Albedo's birthday was yesterday!" Dawn muffled words come out as she continues scarfing down the porridge.

"Yeah, what about it?" Urania shakes her head in confusion, gesturing toward the satyr while looking at Zua. The changeling shrugs and both turn to the bard.

"We still need to get her a gift!" Dawn's eyes are fully wide and staring daggers at her friends. They had completely forgotten that their first mission, above anything else, was to repay Albedo for her kindness and treat her to something for her special day.

"Do you think that weird shop is open?!" Urania lifts herself up, hurriedly making her way to the door with Zua and Dawn following behind her.

"Only one way to find out." Zua beats one of her fists into her palm.

The three exit Quasar's Inn, with newfound vigor and a quest they cannot refuse.

◆

The trio feels like moths being drawn to the faint, warm, flame-like glow of the windows of the rundown shop in the alley. The board that was previously propped up was now smashed to pieces at the doorstep. A sense of uneasiness rolls over Dawn as she sticks out her hand to open the door.

"What if Twilight actually has something better?" The satyr pulls back at the last second, turning to face her companions behind her. They didn't look enthused by the bard's lack of resolve now.

"We were just there yesterday and only saw adventuring things," Zua says in a hushed voice. "So unless you want to get her nothing, I recommend you open that door."

"What are you afraid of?" Urania puts her hands on her hips.

"I just don't think that anyone might be here," Dawn tries to find better words than "I'm scared" to try and get out of going inside.

"Well, the light's on this time." Uraina reaches for the doorknob and twists it, pushing the door open. "So, someone is obviously here now. Plus, the door is unlocked."

"The door was unlocked last time too." Dawn whimpers softly, as both the others walk past her into the dusty store.

Inside, the store seems very much the same, except for the multiple lanterns that are hanging up on the walls, now lit to fill the room with light and shadows. Urania and Zua begin to look around, now being able to see better. Dawn makes her way to the counter to try to find the owner and talk to them. The counter had no one behind it though. Just a single bell and a wooden puppet toy are laying on top of it.

"Guys," Dawn whispers loudly, "no one is here!"

"Did you check in the back?" Zua calls out, picking up a broken accordion, which makes a sad glissando as it sags to the floor.

"I'm not snooping behind the counter!" Dawn replies, still trying to conceal her voice.

"How about the bell?" Urania pops her head out from behind one of the piles, wearing a dirty pirate hat and eyepatch. "There is a bell, right?"

"Yeah." Dawn feels a tear stream down her face. She didn't like that she had to do anything alone in the creepy place while her friends goof off with the random junk. She lifts her hand to the bell, nervously shaking.

Here goes. I can do this. It's just a bell. It's just a bell in a normal store.

A rough-looking teddy bear with a missing button eye falls from the hole in the ceiling. It lands in one of the piles next to Dawn, but slides down, taking a bunch of other items with it. This, of course, scares the girl tremendously. As she lets out a yelp, her hand collides with the bell on the counter, and the ring echoes violently throughout the entire room and into the portal above. Even after all that noise and commotion though, nothing seems to happen.

"Why did you scream?" Zua calls out, rummaging through a pile of garbage, still looking for the perfect gift for a child.

"Because something fell, and it scared me!" Dawn yells back to her unconcerned friend. At that moment, Dawn felt the presence that she was terrified of.

It felt like someone was watching not just her, but her very soul deep within her. Like two murky eyes full of poison and foulness were trying to contaminate her from the inside out. Chills race down her spine, and the hairs on her legs stand up straight.

A small wooden arm creaks as it places itself on her shoulder. It isn't heavy, but the idea of something being behind her now completely drove her to wanting to scream again. Dawn slowly turns her head to look at whatever was now lurking next to her, only to be met with a giant cheshire smile.

"Hello there!" Standing on top of the counter top now is the wooden puppet.

He has mismatched colored eyes, the left being painted orange and right is a bright cyan. A scruffy mat of white hair lay on his head, and his clothes resemble that of a classic jester in red and black leather. He isn't larger than two feet and is hanging from wires coming from the portal.

"Welcome! To Mishaps and Misfortunes!" The puppet lifts up off the counter and into the air, spinning around with his arms stretched out wide.

"Guys!" Dawn shouts, falling to the ground, only to be caught by Urania. Both the barbarian and rogue were making their way over after hearing the new voice ring out into the atmosphere.

"Say!" The puppet swings forward, still levitating, getting very close to Zua's face. "What's your name, Champ? What can I do ya for?"

"Um"—Zua gulps loudly, unable to process the strangeness she is witnessing—"I'm Zua. We're looking for a gift for a friend?"

"A friend?! HAHA!" The puppet spins his head in a full circle, cackling to himself. "Well, aren't you a good person! What a lucky friend!"

"Are you the owner of this shop?" Urania asks, helping Dawn back to her feet. "Dubs, was it?"

"Dobs." Dawn keeps her eyes planted on the puppet, trying to detect what kind of magic was making him act on his own.

"Right," Urania says, shaking her head and hands in front of her, "I didn't mean to be offensive."

"None taken! HAHA!" the puppet chuckles again, quickly moving in front of the demon girl. "And that's my name alright! Don't wear it out!"

"Great"—Zua takes a step back, a little uneasy—"then you can probably help us. We're looking for a toy for a kid. Can we make a deal?"

Dobs' eyes light up almost like they were made of fire. His head violently cranks to look in the direction that Zua was standing, making a loud wooden pop as it does. Zua watches as the already comically large smile carved on his face appears to grow bigger with delight.

"A DEAL?!" Dobs' voice shakes the entire building. "A deal, you say?! Boy, howdy have you come to the right place!"

The puppet flies over behind the changeling in the blink of an eye. He wraps his stubby wooden arms around her shoulders as best he can. Zua feels the tiny hands rubbing on her as if he was trying to massage her to put her in an eased mind state, even if it was doing the exact opposite.

"Great." Dawn smiled nervously before giving Urania a glare of frustration. Her eyes speak to her every word.

This make you happy? Does the weird puppet guy make you happy?

"But first!" Dobs lets go of her and pats Zua on the back. "Why not I offer you my conditions in helping you!"

"Conditions?" Zua tries to look over her shoulder at the abomination in the eyes, but the wooden man pops over to the opposite shoulder instead.

"That's right!" Dobs pushes her forward into Urania, who catches and spins her around to face the living doll. "So let me just fill you in on my sad life story!"

"We didn't ask for that," Dawn nervously pipes in, but Dobs ignores her and hovers over back to the counter, beginning his recount of the story of his tragic past.

"I ain't just any normal salesman, you see! I come from a place far beyond this mortal world, Magnetar, you see! I make deals with mortals for a living delivering their hopes and dreams, but I messed up and made one wrong move, which landed me here on this world with this cursed body! But I still have all my skills and can even cut you a deal if you're willing!"

Oddly enough, the girls slowly become mesmerized by the strange creature. As they listen, the room begins to warp and shift to match his amazing story. Bright colors, psychedelic in nature, glow and images appear out of nowhere, all while Dobs starts moving around, his strings pulling him in every direction until he's right in Zua's face.

"I just wanna go home where I can be free! Get my body back and be the me I'm meant to be! So find a way to get me back to Magnetar!" Dobs' face is too close for comfort and Zua can see deep into his lifeless pupils. The wooden texture on his face is very apparent to her, and it becomes unnerving to look at for too long.

"Wait a second," Urania breaks in, and Dobs turns his head in her direction, "what deal did you make to punish you?"

"Also"—Dawn raises her hand slightly—"this is kind of one sided. You get something and we get nothing?"

Dobs laughs to himself, placing a wooden hand on Zua's shoulder and stretching the other one to the space behind him. His chuckles begin to rise in pitch, as if he was possessed by a demon.

"Oh," he replies, "that's none of your business! And you're right, I am asking for a lot, but it's not just out of the kindness of your heart, see! You want insurance to make sure I hold up my side of the bargain? What smart kids!"

His body starts spinning rapidly, blurring his features so he becomes unrecognizable, propelling him over to his countertop again.

"How about for now you are able to name prices for items in my store and I barter with you for them?" Dobs's smile seemingly grows twice as large while he rubs his hands together.

"And furthermore, once you have a direct line to Magnetar for me, I'll give you my entire store and all its contents free of charge!"

Urania and Dawn's eyes glow with the idea that Dobs lays on the table, but Zua takes time to weigh the options.

"You want to be free from everything in this world? That's a little suspicious." Zua steps up to the counter, glaring at the puppet now. "So, what are you really after?"

Dobs continues to smile, but the grin plastered on his face shifts and turns to a frown with teeth still being barred. His wooden body begins to creak and twitch, and a low rumble of irritation emanates from him. His eyes glint, as he slowly leans over the table, breathing

YUMA

heavily in Zua's face. The barbarian nervously leans back but doesn't lose her ground or footing.

"I just want to go home," Dobs's voice was lower, serious, and seemingly upset now. "Do we have a deal or not?"

Zua turns around to the other two for some assistance, only to be met with Urania making a slicing motion with her hands. Silently, her lips form words that echoed in Zua's head.

Cut his strings.

The changeling turns around to face the merchant again, now giving off an aura of malice. She immediately closes her eyes and breathes heavily. Why was she scared again? What was this creature, and was it a good idea to take his deal or not? Then just as quickly as his attitude changed, Dobs was back to being perky and excited.

"Wonderful! Pleasure doing business with you kid!"

Zua opens her eyes to find that the puppet's hand was gripping hers and shaking it fiercely. Dobs returns to his place behind the counter. He rubs his hands together and laughs for a moment before disappearing into the sea of garbage.

"Zua, you okay?" Dawn asks as she and Urania walk up close to their friend, whispering quietly so they aren't overheard. Dawn grabs the changeling by the face and begins to examine her.

"Why didn't you cut the strings?" Urania asks. "He wants to go home, right? Maybe those strings are holding him here."

"I'm fine." Zua pushes the satyr off of her and faces the demon. "And I couldn't . . . I just."

Zua takes a moment to think about what had happened. She closed her eyes and couldn't move. Just looking at him made her paralyzed. Furthermore, she didn't—no, more likely, *couldn't*—move her hand or arm up to accept his deal. So how did it happen?

"I don't think that would have been a good idea."

The three hear a loud crash and bang from behind the counter, drawing their attention to see what had happened. Just as they do, Dobs pops his head out from the trash, smiling as always. Next, two small objects peek out from near his face, being raised up by his hands.

ODD ENCOUNTERS

"Now that we have our deal"—the puppet laughs—"how about a token of my appreciation! I call it BOGO!"

"Bogo?" The three ask in unison while the shopkeeper places two toys on the counter.

"Buy one, get one! I'm sure it'll be a great hit in the future off sales! HAHA!"

The two toys were worn on two different extremes. The first was a doll with blonde curly hair and a blue dress. It had little brown shoes and rosy pink cheeks. Its smile is faint, and its eyelids were weighted so when it was laying down they closed over the sapphire eyes. The down side was that it was covered in dirt, dust, and possibly blood stains.

The other was a teddy bear, or what was left of one. One of the eyes and arms were missing, with stuffing coming out of the shoulder. The other black button eye was hanging from a thread. Besides all of that, it still seemed cute, with its tongue slightly sticking out of the side of its mouth, and a small little nose and snout.

"I'll sell these once in a lifetime items to you for three thousand gold!" Dobs grins proudly, waving his hands over the toys to add some showmanship to his sale.

"What?!" Urania chokes while taking a breath. She begins coughing a bit after, as Dawn steps forward to examine the dolls.

"May I?" She asks the merchant, who gestures to her to go ahead. The bard looks carefully at the poor toys and sighs looking up at Dobs.

"These really aren't worth more than a couple of gold."

"Then I'll take that much! Two gold, what do ya say?"

"Well, that's better than three thousand." Zua pats Urania on the back, trying to help her regain her composure.

"Sold!" Dobs smile breaks as he opens his mouth and points inside.

Dawn looks confusedly to Zua for help, but the barbarian shrugs and nods. Dawn takes two of her gold pieces out of a small pouch on her hip and puts them inside of the puppet's mouth. Dobs, happily, hands the toys to the satyr and begins to chew the coins with a loud grinding sound.

"So delicious!" He screams in almost pure ecstasy, grabbing the sides of his face and swinging around.

"Well, thank you, I guess." Urania lifts her head, still a bit winded for the sudden unreasonable price for merchandise.

"Anytime!" Dobs chuckles to himself. "Just don't forget our deal! Now, I'm a busy man! Shoo! Scram!"

Without another word, Dobs leaps over the countertop and sticks out his arms. He begins to push the girls toward the entrance and out the door with tremendous speed and force. Once outside, the girls hear him slam the door, which is followed by loud strange whirring sounds and locks being set. Urania reaches for the handle of the door and tries to open it again, only to find that it won't even budge this time. She faces her companions and shakes her head.

"That was the weirdest thing that has ever happened to me," Dawn groaned, putting the toys into her bag.

"That was probably one of the most terrifying things that has happened to me." Zua mimicked Dawn's energy of exhaustion.

A tapping can be heard from the window and the three turn their attention to the shop one last time. In the dust on the window, Dobs is drawing a star shape with the number thirteen next to it. Urania pauses for a moment and tries to think if he was trying to give them a clue to his deal.

Could it be a code or something?

"Urania!" Zua calls out to her from a little further into the alley. "You coming?" Dawn and Zua were a little ways away but still close by for their partner to run to. Urania dismisses her thoughts for now and races to the others, making their way back south towards the Lower Plaza.

✦

Albedo sits in a small wooden throne, cushioned with violet pillows with a few cuts in them, allowing for the stuffing on the inside to leak out. The wood itself is also worn and has marks and notches in it, probably from bladed weapons that were used in a fight in the past. The young goblin watches ahead of her and sees others about her size and age running around, laughing and playing with various toys and prizes they got from the festival.

She looks up at her father, sitting next to her. He is drinking ale straight out of a keg while eating one of the drumsticks that came from the giant cockatrice he brought for the occasion. He laughs while alternating between eating and drinking. Other goblins come up to him and speak to him, either paying their respects or trying to tell him about the hard work they were up to. The young goblin girl then looks down at her hands.

The small doll she is holding has blonde hair and button eyes. A nice green dress made out of cloth was sewn on to make the doll look like a village girl. The child sighs and a small tear runs down her cheek and onto the doll's face. It wasn't that she wasn't thankful for the gift. It was just she didn't have anyone that wanted to play with her. She couldn't really play by herself with just one doll either, the creative mind could only do so much. She drops the doll into the woven basket next to her seat and gets up from the throne to head back to trying to hand out maps to incoming travelers.

"Hey! Albedo!"

A chipper voice calls out over all the noise and excitement. Not only does it gain the little girl's attention, but the rest of the goblins all turn to face the trio of adventurers that were heading their direction. A moment of joy fills the little goblin's heart, and her face beams with excitement seeing Dawn, Urania, and Zua approaching. She turns to her father, eyes wide but not a word spoken. Oort nods and places the keg down onto the ground, getting up from his throne as well. He motions for his daughter to make her way to the group, and Albedo leaps into a sprint.

"Hello, new friends! How are you today?"

The girls awe over the child again, and Dawn pulls out the dolls they had bought from Dobs a few minutes prior. The goblin looks at them in amazement as the satyr places them in her arms.

"We're doing pretty good now that we've got to see you." Dawn smiles lovingly at Albedo, who is dumbfounded at the sight of her doll collection that she is now holding.

"Happy birthday!"

The trio's voices ring out in unison, and Albedo tears up again; this time with a huge smile and a happy giggle. She turns to her father, bouncing up and down. Her face pleading for permission to play with her new toys. Again, Oort nods and extends his arm once more for her to head to a table to his right. The child squeals with excitement and turns to her friends once more.

"Thank you so much! You guys are the best and nicest people I know!"

Without another word, Albedo races to an empty table and places her three toys on top, pretending they are invited to a party and eating food that is on a plate nearby her. Oort chuckles to himself and turns to greet the adventurers.

"Welcome to the Settlement, my friends! What brings ya?"

"We're actually here to talk to you, sir." Dawn stands up again, wrapping her bag around her arm. "Comet sent us to figure out what's going on with you guys and the king."

"Does he now? Well, ain't much to say."

"Fill us in then." Zua's arms cross and she taps her foot on the ground. "I'm a little frustrated with how much Comet isn't telling us. What happened six months ago, start there."

Oort sighs, then takes a large bite out of his drumstick. He points to his throne and begins to walk over to it. The others follow, and Oort motions for the scrawny goblin to join them. Albedo watches everyone gather. Feeling as though something is taking place, she opts out of playing for now and runs back to her chair, placing her new dolls at her side sitting upright.

"Where to start?" Oort strokes his beard with his open hand and sits down with a thud, "Well, for starters, how about the Great King, Ursa Major XV?"

ODD ENCOUNTERS

"He was king over Alpherg for the longest time." The scrawny goblin crosses his arms and closes his eyes, and for a moment it seems as if all his stress evaporates away.

"Before six months ago, things were happy and easy. Goblins and people lived in harmony and there was not an ounce of segregation between humanoids or us goblins. We even were invited to the palace a couple of times to help the king with some matters concerning animals from Carina Forest coming into city limits."

"But that changed when Gibbous took over, right?" Urania scratches her chin, a little puzzled by the abrupt change.

"Well, ya see," Oort places a hand on his smaller goblin friend's shoulder, almost looking like a giant was going to pick him up and swallow him, "King Ursa Major ended up passing away of old age. Somehow, that reached the ears of a couple of adventurers who took that opportunity to swipe the crown of the royal family and sail away with it."

"The prince didn't want to take over without the family heirloom, right?" Zua asks.

"Exactly." The scrawny goblin opens his eyes, now with a saddened expression on his face. "Not only did his father die, but his only remaining piece of him and the symbol of Alpherg was gone too. He couldn't take the pressure, and no one has seen him since."

"That's when the big meanie king was crowned." Albedo's cheeks puff up and her nose scrunches tightly. "He wasn't mean right away, but he was always angry and a bully to everyone."

"How do people continue to serve him, let alone not try and usurp the throne like he did?"

Dawn's comment shocks the goblins, but her friends nod in agreement. If it was true that he was just a terrible king to everyone, even his own men, someone surely must have had the thought to take his place or at least attempt to assassinate the man.

"Well." The small goblin looks up to his boss, his ears drooping a little bit more.

"I've seen it firsthand." Oort shakes his head. "Even if he is a terrible man, something with the guards makes 'em loyal to him, ya know? Due to that, people fear the guards, meaning no one is gonna get close to him without him knowing."

"The guards are very scary now too." Albedo inches closer to her father's leg, latching on and squeezing tightly as though she were afraid. "They have a bad look in their eyes."

Dawn squats down and pats the child on the head, reassuring her a bit. It was obvious that the goblins had ideas and theories, but they didn't know very much compared to everyone else they had spoken too. The satyr stands up again and turns to her friend, but out of the corner of her eye she sees a peculiar sight.

At the foot of the goblin's settlement was a bigger goblin with gloves and a small hat on his head. He is shirtless and has bulging muscles similar to Oort's. A large wolf-like creature is walking beside him, huffing and puffing clouds of dust up off the ground. The creature was twice the size of any wolf Dawn had seen before; a warg. However, the more concerning thing was that behind them are three guards all with weapons drawn and approaching the settlement at a steady pace.

"What the!?" The scrawny goblin steps out in front of Albedo and Oort. "That's Terra, our blacksmith, but what is he doing with Alpherg guards?"

"Something's not right." Oort motions for Albedo to get behind him and at a safe distance.

"Long time, no see, Oort buddy!" a familiar voice rings out over the group, as everyone's attention turns to the nearest table to them. There a very well dressed young man in a blue suit is standing on the oak tabletop, with his hands in his pockets, smiling and watching the guards and goblin approach them.

"Well, if ya ain't making a flashy entrance, Comet, my boy." Oort snorts, turning back to the situation on his hands. "Can't imagine they be with ya?"

"Nope." Comet's smile seems a bit inappropriate for the current mood. He looks down to Dawn, Urania, and Zua and waves.

"These guys might be under a charm spell. Mind to take care of them as another test of your abilities?"

The girls glare at the boy, and then at the small group inching closer. Not much could be said at the moment, so they nod and draw out their weapons, daggers and a rapier. Oort steps out in between them, his scimitar already in a battle position.

"Let's try not to kill them, though," Comet's voice rings out again, and Urania flashes him a look. She gazes upon the kid and sees that he was looking down at his pocket watch. Noticing her, he closes it and smiles.

"I think we might be able to get some information from these guys if we tried, but if we can't, we still shouldn't try to kill them. Don't want a bad image, now do we?"

A woman's scream breaks the tension between the two and Urania faces the advancement again. The goblin named Terra was now looming over a female goblin with his fists in the air, preparing to crush her with his sheer power. Without a second, the demon throws her dagger with a flick at the green bulk, stabbing him directly in his side. Terra turns to face the group and chuckles.

"Men!" One of the guards raises his sword in the air. "Forward! Attack the newcomers and capture the goblin leader!"

"Bring it on ya yellow-bellied weaklings!" Oort's voice booms like thunder as he charges straight toward the enemies; Zua follows close behind with Urania and Dawn on her tail.

The barbarian throws her dagger at one of the guards face, but the man is able to swiftly deflect it with his sword. He grins proudly, boasting to himself for such a flawless execution of skill. As his blade drops from his face, he realizes that his confidence was too soon. Zua's dagger was nothing more than a feint; her real objective was to knock him with her hammer.

She pulls the bludgeoning weapon from out behind her back and collides the head of the mallet with the guard's helmet. The clanging of metal on metal rings out, and echoes in the ears of the man standing in front of her. The guard cries out in pain, dropping his weapon and cupping his helmet where his ears are.

"We can't kill them," Zua grumbled to herself, "but at least we can disorient them, right?"

Comet, still standing on the table, smiles and nods, even though Zua couldn't see him. A small giggle escapes from his mouth, which is all Zua needs to hear to assume she is correct. With a swift spin, she delivers another hit at the man's side, dropping him to his knees. She looks over to her left to find that Terra is staring her down, chuckling softly to himself.

"You want some?" Zua beats her chest with her fist and gets in a ready position to charge at the goblin.

"No, little shifter!" Oort sticks a hand out in front of her, spinning his scimitar in his other hand, "I'll be the one to take care of him."

With a nod, Zua turns around and makes her way to her next target, a guard attacking Dawn. Oort raises his blade up to the goblin in front of him and takes a deep breath in. Terra roars loudly and charges at Oort with unbelievable speed, his fist reaching out and embedding itself in Oort's stomach.

"Oort!" Urania, nearby fighting off one of the other guards, witnesses the sucker punch and watches the goblin leader cripple over from pain.

She swipes her daggers in the face of the guard, slicing both of his cheeks, making him cover his face and reel back. Taking her opportunity, the rogue darts in her companion's direction. A large maw appears at her side, and as she turns to face the creature, she feels its teeth dig into her arm and tear away a part of her. The wolf-like creature steps into her line of sight, getting directly in front of her and the two goblins.

"Bad dog." Urania's eyes gleam with rage, putting her twin daggers back at her side, stretching out her fingers from each hand to reveal her dark sharp claws. The warg lunges and Urania responds with her own.

"Why are you guys doing this?" Dawn asks frantically as she parries multiple swings from the guard in front of her. He doesn't respond and continues his assault on her, getting faster and stronger with each attack.

Zua, getting to where her friend was, looks around for something to help immediately. A table that had been cleared before the brawl broke out was standing beside her and a marvelous idea pops into the barbarian's head. She grabs either side of the oak structure and attempts to lift it, but surprisingly it doesn't move, not even a budge.

Frustrated, Zua lets out a loud scream, tensing her muscles, bulging now three times their normal size. A fire burns in her eye, and an ominous red aura surrounds her. Dawn turns for a moment towards the sound, finding Zua over the table. The guard's blade swings down, hitting her chest. The satyr winces and pulls her head back to butt him in the gut, dropping her rapier at the same time.

"That hurt! What's your problem?" Dawn collides her horns with the guards armor, pushing him back a couple of feet. She steps a few feet back herself and pulls out her fiddle from her bag. Sliding the bow across the strings, music fills the air from the bards position as she begins to sing.

"Muscles, muscles! Hear 'em roar! Zua's strength is about to soar! No more time, no more wait! It's time for you to meet your fate!"

A glowing stream of gold simmers like a river from the instrument to the changeling, mixing with the aura already around her. Zua, standing up straight now, looks down at her hands and then the table that was giving her problems. She grabs one of the legs, pulling it up with the greatest of ease over her head. With a darted glare, the empowered warrior hurls the heavy wooden table with not a sweat.

The guard turns, seeing the impromptu attack too late, and tries to block his face. He lets out a scream of terror as the table explodes into splinters as it makes contact with him, sending him flying backward into the ground with a pile of rubble. The two girls celebrate for a moment with a crisp high-five. Comet, watching the whole event unfold, chuckles, bewildered by the sheer force and wits of his team.

A loud yelp comes from the wolf creature as Urania dives underneath it, biting at one of its legs. Taking her dagger back out, she swipes it down the center of the creature, tearing through its skin. Sliding out from under it, she turns and glares at the monster, exuding a pressure like no other. The warg whimpers and begins to back away slowly, before turning tail.

Urania grabs her arm, blood trickling from her wound. She fights the pain and turns to see how Oort was doing. The goblins were now exchanging barehanded blows to each other, one after another. It was miraculous to watch each impact as the other stumbled but regain his stance and go in for another strike. Eventually, Terra grabbed something from his side; a small vial of a pink substance.

Comet, realizing the danger, grabs his watch and leans forward. The next instant, he's behind Oort in the air. He clicks the button on his watch as Terra looks up in surprise at the teleporting child.

"Close your eyes, Oort, and aim for his jaw!" Comet yells, giving Oort only a second to respond.

Hoping that his friend has complied with his remark, Comet casts a spell around himself. The light draws everyone else's attention to him, as it intensifies and glows brighter like the sun. Dawn, realizing the magic at hand, covers Zua's eye and closes her own.

"Blinding Flare!" Comet yells again, now with the intense light surging like a wave out of his body. Terra, not given enough time to respond, witnesses the minor supernova flash in front of him, causing his vision to go dark.

"Now!"

Oort hears the boy's instruction and the painful screams from Terra and throws his fist in the last place he saw the goblin's face. A loud impact and crack booms, followed by a thud of a body hitting the ground. Everyone opens their eyes to see the four intruders lying on the ground, unconscious and defeated. Comet lands on the ground, spinning around and striking a pose.

"Alright! That's how it's done!" The boy claps loudly and grins from ear to ear.

He nudges Oort in the side, still smiling, trying to lift his friend's mood for the victory. The goblin looks down at the blue boy and begins to laugh, slowly getting louder with each chuckle until the both of them are holding their stomachs and bellowing in joy.

The three girls make their way to the other two but are pushed aside by little Albedo running to her father with tears of joy in her eyes.

"My papa's the best!"

The girls join the group and watch the goblin father lift his daughter up in his arms. Comet turns to face everyone and clears his throat.

"Well, that was fun. How's everyone doing?" He looks at Dawn and Urania who had taken a hard hit each, and reels back his laughter.

"Could be better." Dawn frowns and looks down at her hooves, gently rubbing her wound. Urania was doing the same and looking away from Comet.

"I see." Comet took out his watch again, this time sticking out his other hand at the injured party and clicking the button. "This should help a little. Minor Healing!"

With his words, the two girls watch as green energy pour from his fingertips directly onto their wounds. Shortly after, the gaps began to close and the blood stopped flowing, healing almost perfectly. They both look up in awe at the child, who was putting his trinket back in his pocket and smiling proudly.

"Are you a wizard?" Urania asks, getting in Comet's face with her intense glare. The boy felt a bead of sweat run down his face to his chin, while he stuck his hands out in front of him to make a barrier between the demon and himself.

"No, his magic is too scattered," Dawn said, rubbing her chin and tapping her hoof. She looks directly at Comet with an unblinking stare.

"Oh yeah?" Comet's voice rattles, while his prideful grin turns timid.

"You just used a couple of druid class spells," Dawn continues, not breaking her glazed over expression. "But we've seen him use Laughter on me, which can only be learned by bards and wizards. How do you do it?"

"I'm just lucky I guess." Comet shrugs nervously and takes a step back into Oort. He looks up and feels Oort put his hand on his shoulder.

"Whatever Comet is doesn't matter, ya hear?" Oort smiles down at the boy, "He's a good lad, and he's helped us once again! Along with all of ya! Thank ya, once more, from the bottom of my heart."

"No problem." Zua rubs the bottom of her nose, puffing up again.

"Anyway," Comet looks back to the girls, "let's get down to business. I came here to tell you guys that things are on their way. We'll be able to fix this problem very soon, by the end of the day to be exact."

"What problem?" Albedo asks from up above everyone else.

"The problem with King Gibbous." Comet grins mischievously at the goblin child and then turns to the trio again. "I know I sent you here to do your own investigation, but I talked to one of my friends here at the Shrine of Draco and he filled me in."

"So we did all of this for nothing?" Urania and Zua sigh, looking at each other and then at Comet with anger.

"Not necessarily," Dawn pipes up again, smiling and lifting a finger, "because if we weren't here talking to the goblins, no one would have been around to help them take on the ambushers."

"Excellent point!" Comet laughs, rubbing the back of his head out of embarrassment that he needed help to justify why they were there, since he wasted their time.

"You get a pass for now," Zua growled, "but tell us what you're talking about, please. No more secrets than what's already on the table."

"That's fair," the boy responds. "So here's what I got. Gibbous is using charm magic to make the guards loyal to him. He plans on sending them to ambush the goblins and drive them out of the city, dead or alive."

Albedo tucks her face into Oort's shoulder, and he consoles her. Comet smacks a fist into his palm and smiles again.

"However, they will be preparing this ambush near their barracks at the palace in about an hour from now, which leaves the palace with less enough men to keep the king safe from our own ambush!"

"Brilliant thinking, boy!" Oort cocks a menacing smile. "'Bout time someone gives ol' Gibbous some of his own medicine."

"So we're storming the castle?" Zua asks, unimpressed with Comet's plan. "Just the four of us?"

"Actually, we already have had men on the inside undercover for a good while now apparently," Comet boasts for a moment, standing a little taller now. "And they are all from the Draco Clan here in the city. So we have not only us, but a whole group of druids able to shapeshift into dragons."

"Dragons!" The trio's eyes light up with different expressions; Dawn being concerned, Urania with wonder, and Zua filled with excitement.

"Yeah," Comet laughs, knowing he finally was getting to them, "so what I want you to do next is get ready for the biggest battle that Alpherg has ever seen. Get supplies and some rest, and then meet me in front of Alpherg Palace in one hour."

Without another word, the boy starts walking away, and disappears into the crowd outside of the goblin's area. The girls look at each other, excitement brewing in the air.

"Let's head back to the inn for now, rest, and come up with a plan of what we need," Dawn suggests, the others nodding in agreement. They wave goodbye to their goblin friends and start making their way back to the Central Plaza.

"We'll probably want better armor," Zua tells Urania, "figuring how well that last fight went."

"Yeah," Dawn says, butting into their conversation, "but Comet might be able to heal us again if need be."

"I don't know," a higher pitched voice breaks through the air from underneath them. "How can we trust that guy?"

"He's definitely hiding something, that's for sure," another voice remarks, this one with a slight lisp.

"Yeah, but he did save Apogee that one time, so maybe we should give him a chance," one more strange voice, low and muttering, speaks up.

Zua looks down to see that three strange creatures were walking in the middle of their group. A lighter toned one with two tendrils on it with eyeballs on the ends, a darker one with a large runny nose, and a stubby one with a tongue hanging out of its mouth.

"So that means that we owe him our help for helping Apogee," the big-nosed one with the low voice continues.

"That makes sense, I guess," the stammering large-tongued creature nods in agreement.

"Well," the lighter one with the higher voice grumbles, "let's not get too attached. Gotta slip away if any real danger happens, or we'll end up like Apogee."

This creature's eyes shift up to stare directly at Zua. Now the whole group was looking down at the trio of small grotesque beings. None of them were clothed, and mucus seemed to be dripping from their bodies. It becomes more intense as everyone sits and stares at each other. Finally, the lighter one points at the girls and lets out a horrific scream. The three creatures dash away, fleeing at a breakneck speed that could only be called supersonic.

"What was that?" Urania tilts her head to the side.

"I don't know, but I need a drink." Zua hunches over and continues walking.

The group eventually makes their way to Quasar's Inn. Stepping inside they are met with the smell of delicious spices and broths cooking on the fire in the kitchen. They sit down at an empty table and flag down a waiter for some of the soup. Dawn looks out the window, trying to rack her mind on who those creatures they met could have been. She had sworn she ran into something similar in the Fey Realm.

CHAPTER 4

Siege on Alpherg Palace

Broth from Quasar's beef and potato soup streams down Zua's face as she shovels the contents into her mouth, as if she wasn't planning on eating ever again. She pauses momentarily to chug on a pint of ale and then continues to devour the meal along with a loaf of bread sitting beside her bowl. Her eyes meet with Urania's, who is watching disappointedly from across the booth.

"What?" The changeling shrugs her shoulders, ripping a piece of bread with her teeth and chewing it about three times before swallowing.

"We have an hour to be ready for this mission and you decided to order five different things!" The demon girl points down to the table, littered with empty bowls and plates. It was evidence of Zua's wrath of hunger.

"We haven't eaten since breakfast!"

"That was only about two hours ago," Dawn calls out from across their booth. She is pacing around with her hand on her chin, staring into the floor as she makes small circles. Zua frowns at the disapproval of her hunger, but continues to eat, but more quietly.

"What's on your mind?" Urania turns to the bard, putting an arm over the booth and facing her. "You've been quiet ever since we found those *things*."

"I just feel like I know what they are." Dawn grabs her horns at the base of her head and squints her eyes closed. "But I don't know where."

The satyr is very well versed in magic and mystical things, being a fey. However, she always has a hard time when she doesn't know something. Her brain begins to race at a mile a second, and her

75

attention doesn't return until she has solved her mystery. Were they fey? It wasn't unlikely, but they were too strange for even fey. Maybe something more?

Suddenly a thought pops in her mind and her eyes light up like the morning sun. Bringing a fist down into her palm in front of her, she lets out a cry of realization, but it is interrupted by a loud ungodly roar. Zua pats her stomach, bulging out of her clothes a little bit, and snickers to herself.

"No better compliment to the chef, am I right?"

Dawn's gaze changes from joyous to anger and rage. Whatever she had thought of has flown out the window, and the last ten minutes have been a waste of her time. She stomps over to the booth and screams at the gluttonous barbarian in a hushed voice.

"I almost had it! And then you had to . . . ARGH!" She sits herself down next to Urania in a violent huff and crosses her arms. She is too upset to try and recall anything and wants to brood in her anger rather than say or do anything else.

"You guys are a little tense right now," Zua grumbles. "What's the big deal anyway?"

"We have less than an hour to get ready for the mission! Don't you remember?"

Zua stares at Urania blankly and then pops back into reality.

"Oh, right. Yeah, I think I'm just going to wing it, you know?"

"Wing it? We're entering the palace of a tyrant king, what do you mean by winging it?" Urania's face scrunches and her hand covers her eyes. With a shake of her head, she relieves herself of the foolish statement she had just heard and clears her throat.

"We need to get some better weapons and armor and then go from there."

"I guess. But what about you Dawn? Don't you need a spell book or something?"

"I know all my spells by heart." Dawn doesn't look up from the ground, still curled up in rage. "I only would need scrolls or books if I was to learn something new."

Her eyes grow and she shoots up out of her seat and pulls off her bag from her back. After shuffling around inside of it for a moment, she pulls out the crude map the girls received from Albedo and unraveled it. Just as she thought, she points to a location with eagerness in her voice.

"There is a library though! I saw it when passing by on our way here. And maybe I should talk to Twilight about the books in her store too!"

"That sounds promising." Urania smiles and turns back to Zua, who is also eyeing some place on the map too. "And what about you? Somewhere you want to go now?"

"No." The barbarian gets up and starts to walk towards the door, giving a waiter a handful of gold pieces on her way. "I think I'll just take a stroll if you guys don't mind? Let's meet at Sidereal's in a half hour and then get some weapons and armor. Then we can go to the palace."

Without another word, Zua walks out the door and heads east towards the Central Plaza area. Urania looks over her shoulder with slight suspicion but sighs and turns back to Dawn. The satyr was packing her map back into her bag and cleaning up Zua's mess on the table.

"Want to head to the library first or Twilight's?" Urania stands up next to her companion, they both start making their way to the exit.

"Oh? You want to join me at the library? Did you have something you wanted to find too?"

"In a way, yeah." The demon flashes her fangs in a smile, gentle yet mischievous. "Every palace has to have a blueprint right, and I'm sure we could use that."

Dawn feels a chill crawl down her spine as she witnesses the evil expression on Urania's face twist. But the smile wasn't directed toward her, which was comforting in a way. The girls walk out into the street and proceed to head southeast of the inn, with Dawn leading with the little bit of general direction she had to their destination.

After a few minutes they arrive at the Alpherg Library. It is a rather small marble building with a few pillars in the front entrance for decoration more than structural support. The roof is flat, except for a giant glass dome that seems to be in the direct center of the building. It is about two stories tall and rather new looking, either that or it was well maintained. But that isn't what caught the girls attention right away. The fact that the building is nice to view was a plus, but the more interesting thing is that there is a long line of people in front of the entrance. They stop for a moment and look at each other in disbelief but press on. They arrive at a stall just before the line starts, where a man is sitting with a large ledger in front of him. He is young, no older than twenty and is human.

"Are you upper class or lower class?" The young man sighs, his head nodding up and down slightly. His eyes have dark rings around them, and his hair is a mess.

"Um, what?" Dawn asks, confused by why he needed such a strange piece of information.

"The library can only hold so many people and with the new laws in place by King Gibbous, we need to take count. Only four commoners in at a time."

"What about the upper class then?" Urania asks, her arms crossing in front of her. Her body was starting to get used to being in this position.

"King Gibbous has stated that if an upper class citizen wishes to browse the library that they are free to do so without any delay. But you'll need identification."

"So, this line is for common folk?" A worried look washes over Dawn. "It's so long, what's the wait time?"

"About three hours give or take." The man yawns and catches his head dropping with a quick neck snap, bringing it back up so he could see the girls.

"No more questions, you obviously aren't upper class so please either get in line or you are free to leave. Thank you for coming to the Alpherg Library."

Urania bites her thumb and looks down at the ground, quickly trying to come up with a lie. But would the guy believe her? He is obviously tired, but his attention was still on his job, and that didn't seem like it was difficult to try and trick him on. What to do? Dawn was hoping to find something, and she wanted to get her hands on a map of at least a layout of the palace before they went in.

She looks up at the man behind the stall again, but to her surprise he is standing up at attention. His eyes are fixed on her hand and with a shift of her eyes Urania comes to understand why. A small star is glowing in blue on her hand, the mark that Comet gave her.

"Do you know Comet?" The young man, still looking very much like he could use a nap, is now filled with energy and life. His eyes dart from Urania to Dawn and then back to Urania.

"Um, yeah?" Not sure what to say the girls agree in unison.

"I'm so sorry for wasting your time! You must be here on his mission. I'll let you in right away."

The hushed whispers of the man were a bit confusing, but neither of the two were going to argue with his gesture. They follow him straight up to the front of the line, where two guards are posted. One of them raises a hand up to the girls and turns to the man who nods toward the guard before leaving swiftly. Without any words, they move aside and allow the satyr and demon to walk through.

Inside, the library was rather small but filled with shelves, lined like stalls at a market. Books of all shapes, colors, and sizes are squeezed together on every one of the levels of the wood shelves. The maze of literature would have been imposing to any random person walking in, but no one could be more of an expert in a library than Dawn.

The satyr's eyes sparkle and shine like stars, as she slowly walks into the main corridor. A single desk stands between her and the horde of knowledge. A young elf with white hair and blue eyes notices her and Urania from behind the desk. He walks around and quickly towards them, with arms outstretched.

"Welcome to the Alpherg Library!" His voice was gentle and deep for his appearance. He looks rather young but a few lines on his face reveal that he could be very much older than them both combined.

"Thank you." Urania leans forward slightly and awkwardly, not sure if she should show respect or not. "We are happy to browse through your selections if you don't mind."

"Yes," the elf laughs, a little confused, "that is what most people do in the library. However due to recent turmoil in the city, we can't allow any of the books to leave the premises for fear of being stolen or destroyed. On further note, anything on the top floor must not be taken off the shelves and viewed without supervision. Enjoy."

He begins to walk back behind the desk when Dawn snaps back to reality. She attempts to grab his sleeve, falling short a little. With a clearing of her throat, to regain her composure, he turns back to face them.

"You wouldn't happen to have any fairy tales or folk stories, would you?" Dawn's nervous smile reflects easily to the elf, and he smiles happily.

"A bit of a storyteller yourself, are you?" He extends a hand out in front of him and starts to lead them down a walkway. "Right this way."

Excitedly, Dawn follows with Urania trailing behind. The demon keeps her eyes peeled for anything unusual or important looking that might help her get an idea of the next challenge they were about to face.

She believes that with information you can find secrets and hidden treasures that would normally be right underneath one's nose. However, nothing she saw seemed like it would be of any use. Romance novels, books of recipes for both food and potions, there were even books on magic and how to use it, but nothing on the palace itself.

"Here is our folk story and bizarre fantasy tales section."

The elf stopped in front of a shelf about five feet tall with many markers in it, each signifying a different type of genre that someone could be looking for. The section he pointed out was no more than about thirty books wide, and as Dawn quickly ran her finger over the spines, her smile turned to a frown.

"What's wrong?" Urania asked, puzzled by the girl's reaction. "There's plenty of stories here."

"Not if you've read them all. I know each of them by heart." Dawn slumped her shoulders in defeat and gently bumped her head on the bookshelf.

"If that's the case"—the elf clears his throat—"maybe you should think of heading to Bellatrix. It is known for being a magic school city, sure, but they have every book ever printed in their libraries."

"Bellatrix you say?" Urania scratches her chin and looks at Dawn, who was still moping.

"Do know that you need a reason for entering the city though. Some say the blue woman who runs the supply store in town sometimes writes letters of entry." With that said the elf man smiles and walks away.

"That sounds like Twilight." Urania smacks her fist into her palm, getting a bit excited for Dawn.

"Now that he said it"—the satyr lifts her head—"I remember seeing a paper in Twilight's bookshelf that said something about visiting Bellatrix."

"We should pay her another visit then when we're done here." Urania looks around to try and find another person to help her this time, when she notices a very shabby looking young man. She grabs Dawn by the arm and starts pacing towards him.

"Hey, excuse me," Urania says before even getting to the man, who seems very terrified by her approach.

Maybe it was the fact that she wasn't very quiet, or that she wasn't being her most polite self, or possibly that she was a half-demon. But when she got around to thinking about it, it was probably a combination of all three reasons.

"Yes?" The young man's voice quivers and his knees shake. He clasps the book he is holding close to his chest, as if it was to be his defense against her.

"We were wondering if you work here, and if you could help us." Urania takes a breath, and reconsiders her approach, becoming gentler.

"I do," the man replies. "What are you needing help with?" He looks down at Urania's tail, which is wagging slowly against the ground. He gulps, as he notices the spaded tip looks rather sharp, enough to probably impale him.

Urania sighs internally, knowing full well that the man isn't going to be much use unless she could think of something quick. Her eyes scan about him, trying to find something to use to her advantage. Finally, something came to mind, and she went with her scheme.

"I couldn't help but notice that you are reading some books on architecture." She points to the book that he was holding, and the man's face becomes red.

"Yeah," the man chuckles nervously, but it is more of a guilty awkward laugh than one of terror. "I happen to be a big know-it-all about buildings and structures. It's a useless hobby, really."

Dawn looks to Urania, who in response winks at her. She leans in closer and wraps herself around his arm. Dawn's face bursts into a beet red flush, and she hides her face in her hands.

"Then you're just the guy I need!" Urania giggles, pressing up against the young man's arm.

"Oh? With what?" the man's voice cracks a bit, and he takes another big gulp. His face is also becoming very red.

"We would like to see the blueprints for Alpherg Castle. We figure that they should be stored in the library for safe keeping." Urania bats her eyes at him and smiles innocently.

"I myself am also a big nut for buildings and structures. I like to know what makes each one unique."

"Do you mean Alpherg Palace?" The young man gives her a puzzling look, and she quickly turns to Dawn for help. The satyr is still too embarrassed though to return to reality.

"Yes," Urania speaks slowly, searching for her words. "I was just using the old term for it that my mother told me about? When I was a kid?"

The face of uncertainty looks down on the demon, who slowly begins to release the man's arm. She would have been so close if she hadn't messed up with a single mistake, how careless and sloppy.

That was such a good lie too, and the chance to use it again would be too long for her to care.

"Incredible!" The man cheers loudly, and then brings his hands over his mouth. He looks around to make sure no one was disturbed by his outburst, then turns to face Urania and Dawn again.

"I can't believe I found someone who knows such an uncommon fact. It was the Castle of Alpherg until it was changed to Alpherg Palace by the late king's grandfather, Ursa Major XIII, and has remained like that even with King Gibbous on the throne. Though I hear he wants to rename it to Castle of Glorious Gibbous."

Dawn peeks out from between her fingers and catches a glimpse at Urania. The demon shrugs her shoulders, and Dawn lets out a sigh of disbelief.

"So then," Urania smiles again, "would it be too much to ask to see the layout plans? Pretty please?"

"Well, it's not information that is generally public knowledge," the young man rubs the back of his neck, "but on the other hand..."

"On the other hand?" Dawn finally speaks up, confused why the whole plan her companion cooked up was actually working ironically well.

"On the other hand, it's upstairs and you need supervision. That means that I'll be there the whole time, plus like I said, not a lot of people ask about it, so it's not like it's supposed to be kept secret, I think?"

"Then we can go as long as you show us and we don't touch anything, right?" Urania's smile grows wider. She looks to Dawn for help again, and the satyr finds that she has no choice but to smile too.

"Okay." The man laughs awkwardly. "Follow me." The girls follow behind the poor man, with Dawn in complete confusion as to what just happened.

The trio climbs the spiral staircase in the center of the bottom floor all the way to the top. The roof was partially open in the center with a glass dome skylight as the only source for illumination. The bookshelves on the top floor were similar to the ones on the lower level, except for one thing.

"Why are the books locked up like prisoners?" Dawn asks genuinely. Each of the cases has glass sliding doors and locks on the fronts of them, seemingly to keep the books from escaping their confinement.

"It's to make sure no one takes them," the man returns Dawn's curious remark with a raised eyebrow.

"They are not prisoners, it's simply to keep important documents, like the one we're going to look at, safe from nefarious people."

The satyr gives Urania a side eyed glance, as if to say that she was a nefarious person. Urania plays along, pretending to be offended by the accusations the look imposes on her. The two share a smile, but quickly resume their roles as they stop in front of one of the cases. The young man pulls out a ring of keys from his pocket and proceeds to open the case and pull out an old dusty leather book.

"These are the schematics for everything that is Alpherg Palace." The man wipes off a bit of the dust from the cover of the book as he walks over to one of the tables. "So, what are you looking for?"

"Anything really." Urania leans in close again to the attendant, this time only to get a good look at the book. "I'm really not sure if there's anything in particular that I'm looking for."

"Oh . . . Well." The man rubs his neck again, a little flustered that the girl is super close to him again.

As the two peer over the blueprints, Dawn walks around looking at some of the cases. She figures she shouldn't stray too far, but her curiosity for why the knowledge needs to be locked up was getting the best of her. It isn't until she comes to one of the cases that seems to be empty that she decides she's seen enough. As she turns to leave, she stops in her tracks, feeling an icy breeze coming for the locked case.

"You seek something child . . . But you know not yet what it means."

The bard turns back toward the bookcase and takes a step back in confusion. The shelves were empty, but now they were filled with books, blue and with gold writing on them reading the same thing,

The Star of Dreams. She reaches out to touch the case, unknowingly, and her eyes change from brown to a starry blue.

"Hey! You can't touch the cases," the man shouts from across the room. He startles Dawn and she turns to face him. "Even if there aren't any books in them, it's still good to not break the rules laid out."

Empty? The satyr, confused, looks back at the case. Sure enough, the bookcase is empty again. Dawn backs away slowly, not taking her eyes off of the weird wooden contraption until she returns to the table where the other two are.

"So, as you can see, the entire palace's structure is still the way it was when King Ursa Major XIII came to power. The only thing he ever did to the building was change its name. If you want older records of the Castle of Alpherg when it was first built, we will have to go back to the era of King Ursa Major VII!"

It is very obvious that the attendant is knowledgeable on what he is telling Urania, but the demon girl kept her eyes fixed on the blueprints in front of her. In her mind, she is taking in all the information down to the number of arches in each hallway, until something catches her eye.

"Like any great kings." Urania grins mischievously. "There's always a secret escape lined up in case of emergency."

She points to a small tunnel that was drawn in faintly underneath the lines of the building. It led from the throne room and royal bedroom to an exit a few yards away from the palace itself. The attendant looks at her with confusion and worry on his face, and Dawn nudges her in the side to say something.

"I just," Urania stumbles to find an excuse that isn't too unbelievable, "love the loyalty that architects have toward their rulers. This one clearly saw the king's life as valuable enough to give him a way out if anyone stormed in?"

Her voice trails off into a higher pitch as the expression of the man goes from concerned to suspicious in a matter of seconds. He grabs the furthest end of the book and closes it, pulling it close to him as he slowly makes his way back to the shelf to put it back. He doesn't release his gaze from the two girls for a single moment.

"Nice one," Dawn whispers, hitting herself in the head.

"I was under pressure," Urania quips back. "And he was bound to find out we were up to something."

The young man locks the case and walks back to the table, a little hurriedly now. He leans over it and whispers softly to the girls.

"Okay, something is up with you two. Why did you really want to see those schematics? Please tell me you're not going to do anything crazy with that information."

"Well," Dawn sighs, unable to hold in the tension feeling that keeping the truth from someone has brought her, "we're actually going to meet up with a group soon to see if we can dethrone this tyrant king of yours."

It was Urania's turn to slap herself in the face. The attendant looks up to the demon as if to ask if her friend was telling the truth. A moment passes and the man smiles and giggles to himself.

"That's wonderful news!" he exclaims quietly, pounding the table softly with his fist.

"With Gibbous out of the picture, I'm sure things will go back to normal, and the library can get its expansion contract approved."

"Wait, what?" Urania turns to Dawn, amazed that her truthfulness actually brought them an ally rather than an enemy.

"You see," the young man continues, "Gibbous has been greedy and horrible when it comes to the resources of Alpherg. It's not just the library, but the goblins are facing discrimination, and there's talk that he wants to get rid of them entirely."

"We know about that." Dawn nods her head. "Some of our goblin friends have already been attacked."

"I had the idea to try and figure out if Gibbous could escape from the palace," Urania spoke up again. "And if he can, then I don't know if we'd be able to get him and save the goblins."

"Luckily for you, Gibbous is prideful." The attendant winks with a smile and snaps his fingers. "The old bastard hasn't left that palace in six months, and something tells me he won't want to give up his throne so easily."

"I'm glad we still got a look at things. Thank you."

Urania sticks out her hand to the young man, and he blushes. Nervously, he grabs a hold of it and shakes. Without another word, the rogue and bard turn towards the stairs and start making their way back to the ground level. The attendant is left upstairs by himself for a moment, and out of joy he leaps into the air and starts cheering softly to himself again.

◆

Zua pulls out her map that Albedo had drawn up and given to the group. It was poorly scribbled together and almost impossible to read, but most of the landmarks were in the right places. She follows it all the way past the fountain and up to Twilight's Supplies.

"Okay." She sticks her thumb in her mouth and looks around for a moment.

"If I'm here, then that means I just need to go southeast?"

Pulling the map up again, she follows her intended path with her finger to a marking that looks difficult to distinguish. It looks like a white blob with blue eyes and horns all over its body. The changeling sighs, folds up her map, and takes a deep breath in before committing to her decision.

After a little bit more walking she comes to a large marble pantheon-like structure with massive pillars supporting the entrance. It is difficult to see, but Zua could make out something inside. A statue stands in the center, sitting on a tall pedestal. White bat wings spread out wide, and sparkling sapphire stone eyes tempt the barbarian to come closer.

"Shrine of Draco!" A grand smirk sweeps across Zua's face as she nods to herself pleased that she was able to find it.

She notices, standing a good distance in front of the entrance, two men in sandy colored robes with their arms behind their backs. They have long silvery hair and light blue eyes like a clear sky. Curious, Zua takes a few steps forward, approaching them at a steady pace.

"Good morning, sirs!" Zua says professionally, as if she were going to try and sell something to the men,

SIEGE ON ALPHERG PALACE   87

"I came all this way to see this lovely shrine of yours. I'm a fan of dragons you see and just could help from hearing about it."

The men stand still, not even acknowledging her in the slightest.

"Okay, cold shoulder." Zua mopes for a second and regains her resolve by marching forward as if nothing can stop her.

To stop her, the men swiftly move their arms from behind their backs, revealing long wooden staves with a dragon's head carved on the top. Inside of the mouth of the dragon is a large blue crystal that glows faintly with magic. They cross their staves with each other to form a barrier in front of the girl.

"Ahh." Zua stops mid stride and takes a step back. "I see you won't let me pass. Can I ask why?"

"Master Blue is away right now," the man on the left speaks without moving to look at her.

"Please come back again at a later time," the other says to the barbarian in a similar way and tone as the first.

Zua, feeling a little defeated, hunches over a little and sighs.

"Who's this Master Blue? Is that a code name for the Comet guy?"

"No. Sir Comet and Master Blue are two completely different people entirely," the first guard says.

"So, what if I say Comet sent me?" Zua tries the only card in her hand she could think of.

"Impossible," the second replies. "Sir Comet would have informed Master Blue of any planned meeting prior to your visit."

Zua steps back again and the men move their staves to a vertical position at their sides. The changeling looks frustratedly over to the statue and grumbles to herself. It was rather unsatisfying to have the goal within sight and being stopped by someone on your way there.

"Look, guys," Zua attempts to reason with the guards, "I'm only here to check it out. I promise I'll be on my way after I get done looking at it."

"Out of the question. Access denied," they speak in unison and stamp the end of their staves into the ground, surely trying to intimidate her.

"Holy people," Zua scoffs to herself and turns around. However, she immediately turns back around and charges straight towards the shrine.

In an instant, the guards turn around fully with their staves facing outside of their bodies now and extend their arms out to grab the girl. Zua laughs at the thought of their puny mage arms being able to restrain her bulk of barbarian muscle. She feels them grab her arms, and then transform them into large limbs five times their size.

White scales and toned muscles rip through their robes. Sharp claws extend out of their fingers and coil around her arms easily. Without another motion from them, Zua feels her body come to a halt, being flung back slightly by her own momentum. With a turn of their hips, the two men catapult her to the ground, even further away than from where she charged them.

"That is your final warning." The first man's eyes change from being human to lizard-like.

"Your next attempt will cost you your life." The second's teeth become jagged, and from the inside of his mouth white sparks crackle.

From the ground, Zua lifts up her hands to surrender. She gets up and dusts herself off, while the guards revert back to a more human looking state, instead of the amalgamation they used to detain her. With no other options and not wanting to meet whatever fate they had intended for her if she continued to persist, Zua walks away from the shrine. From a safe distance, raises her fists up toward them and shakes them in the guards' direction, sticking her tongue out in the process.

✦

Urania and Dawn swiftly made their way through the Central Plaza, passing by the fountain that forever shall hold a special place in their hearts. Dawn, a little further ahead of Urania, was keeping a fast walking speed while not leaving the demon behind. She really wanted to ask Twilight something, and she could hardly contain the excitement.

Just as the two find themselves at the entrance of the supply shop, a familiar face passes by looking rather depressed; Zua. The three girls stop for a moment and look at each other, each holding a different expression. Zua was moping about due to her failed attempt to get into the dragon shrine she had wanted to, while Urania seemed out of breath after chasing the ecstatic satyr to their destination.

"How was your walk?" Urania asks, taking a couple of tries to get her sentence out past her heavy breathing.

"Don't really want to talk about it." Zua kicks a small stone across the pavement near a building alongside the street Twilight Supplies was on. "How was the library?"

"We managed to learn a little about how the palace is structured," Dawn replies cheerfully, bouncing onto the tips of her hooves. "But besides that it was pretty mundane."

"We're going to talk to Twilight because Dawn here has a question from the last time we visited."

As Urania finishes speaking, she notices the bard has already opened the door and walked inside. The two left in the street shrug at each other and follow the lead of the satyr. The store isn't too different from the last time they visited, but a couple of items were gone while a few clothing pieces were restocked. Across the room, working on one of her items, sits the blue woman the group had come to see.

"Good morning." Twilight kept her eyes fixed on her project. "It's quite a pleasure to see you again."

"We're in a bit of a hurry." Dawn claps her hands together and bows her head respectfully, apologizing for her hoping to be brief questioning. "But can you tell me if you have any more books by chance?"

"Did you check the shelves?" Twilight again doesn't look away from her stitching.

"Yes, but I was hoping you had more in the back? Or have any stories you could tell me?"

"I'm afraid I don't."

Dawn drops her hands and frowns. She figured it was a long shot, but the woman was so cold it felt like she didn't even want to help them.

"Let's go then." Urania pats the satyr on the shoulder for reassurance and starts making her way to the door with Zua. Dawn looks down at the ground for a moment, and then back at the woman behind the counter with fire in her eyes.

"Okay," she sighs. "What can you tell me about Bellatrix?"

Twilight's eyes pop almost out of her head, and the thread she was pulling on snaps. She puts down her work and leans up over the counter, revealing her immense height. Her long, blue, boney fingers wrap around the edge of the countertop, as her face comes close to Dawn's.

"You're interested in going to Bellatrix?" Twilight's tone changes from snobby to curious. "Just for some books?"

"Well." The satyr blushes and scratches her head. "I'm supposed to be going there for school, but I got a little distracted on the way. And now I also have the mission Comet wants me to do too."

A miraculous transformation occurs on Twilight's face. Her usual disinterested expression morphs into one of excitement and glee. She laughs to herself, like a wealthy woman would looking down on a peasant.

"I would have never placed you as a student at the Bellatrix Institute of the Arcane! Tell me, what is your major? Oh, what mansion were you assigned to? How much has changed since my enrollment?"

"Hang on." Urania steps forward, pulling Dawn away from the blue woman's reach. "Do you mean to tell us that you go to that college too?"

"I am indeed an alumnus of Bellatrix," Twilight says proudly, bringing her hand to her chest as though she were posing for a crowd.

"That's great!" Dawn exclaims, breaking free of Urania's hold and stepping closer to the shopkeeper. The two began talking excitedly about magic, the uses and benefits it's had on society, along with a few fun facts about Bellatrix and its history.

"I've never seen anyone freak out so much about a school," Zua whispers to Urania, who was standing in pure shock as to what she was witnessing.

"Bellatrix is not just any school," Twilight snaps back. Her eyes turn to darts and pierce a glare in Zua's direction.

"It is the best school to learn all forms of magic in the whole world! My parents are even alumni, and they're famous in the Fey Realm."

Dawn pulls out a small book from her bag with a brown leather cover. It is worn from use and age, and the pages inside of it are starting to turn yellow in color. She flips through it, passing pages full of handwritten text in black ink and watercolor illustrations that are hand drawn into place. She eventually gets to the center where the book becomes blank and holds it up for Twilight to see.

"I've been keeping my family legacy alive," she says proudly, gleaming eyes looking over the rim of the book. "And I want to add some stories and tales I learn from Sol here in this book. Do you happen to know any on hand?"

Twilight smiles warmly at the girl, almost as though she was feeling nostalgic. The smile quickly turns into a cough and her fixed stern look as she sits back down in her seat.

"Well," she says hesitantly, "I guess you should know a little bit about Sol's history if you're going to be here. How about the story of Zenith the Wish Granter?"

Zua and Urania perk up and move closer to the counter where Dawn was standing. Dawn lowers her book slowly and tilts her head to the side. This was the first time they were hearing anything about a person by that name, let alone how they played a part in Sol's history.

"This is an old tale," Twilight continues, "or as some may say now, a fairy tale. Nevertheless, I'll summarize for you."

Dawn leans in close to listen carefully, closing her book and placing it on the counter under her hand.

"There was once only one star in the night sky, and the world was in dark times. Wars were rampant and hope was lost. Then the people of this island wished on the single star, and from it came Zenith. He was a powerful creature born from their wish who had the power to make anything a reality. He agreed to grant their wishes, but at a request. As long as people made wishes and had dreams, his people could continue living and protect the land from harm."

Urania looks down at Zua, who shrugs and shakes her head. Dawn, on the other hand, had tears building in her eyes, as though the she was moved by the story in some way.

"Or it goes something like that." Twilight waves her hand in the air, dismissing the tale. "It's in a book that holds all of Sol's important stories and tales, but there are only two in existence."

"Where can I find them?!" The words shot out of Dawn's mouth as if she were on fire. Twilight and the others reel back in shock of the tiny satyr's loudness.

"Well, one is on the World of Wishes, Magnetar. The other is somewhere on Sol. Probably one of the other four major cities."

"And those are?" Zua crosses her arms, not really caring about finding the book, but knowing the other important places of the country would be useful.

"Bellatrix in the east, Regulus at the center, Sirius to the west, and Polaris lies up north." Twilight uses her fingers to point in the directions of the cities as she lists them off.

"We wouldn't have to ask if that Comet gave us a map or something," Urania grumbles to herself.

"By the way." Twilight rubs her chin, her eyes squinting as she pulls out a watch from a draw behind her counter. "Shouldn't you all be helping Comet with something? You know, the palace raid?"

"How do you know that?" Dawn asks in awe of Twilight's knowledge.

"He told me to keep you on track. Seems his caution was warranted this time around."

"Shit!" Urania exclaims, completely forgetting that they only had a limited amount of time to prepare before the mission began.

"How much time do we have left?"

"About fifteen minutes."

"That's plenty of time to get to Sidereal's and get some armor and weapons." Zua grabs her two companions by the backs of their collars and starts pulling them towards the exit.

"Bye!" Dawn waves to Twilight. "See you after we dethrone the king!"

The door closes and Twilight snickers quietly to herself. She looks up at where the girl was standing and smiles gently again.

"What an interesting daughter you have, Sage. She's just like you."

◆

The sounds of clanging metal grow louder and louder as the group runs through the streets of the Central Plaza. Zua is the first to reach Sidereal's Forge and attempts to catch her breath before speaking to the massive dwarf.

"Sidereal. Armor. Quick." Zua manages to get her point across through her gasps of air, as the other two follow shortly behind her.

"I was wondering when you would come in." The smith grins, dropping his hammer on the anvil.

He walks over to a wall and starts pulling off some items. The trio trails behind him, Urania and Zua holding their hands above their heads, trying to maximize the breath intake. Dawn takes time to grab one of her legs and stretch it behind her, not feeling winded in the slightest.

"How come you aren't tired?" Urania huffs at the satyr. "We ran almost the entire distance of the Central Plaza."

"Satyrs are born for running." Dawn giggles to herself, stretching out her other leg now.

"The fey have it easy." Zua grumbles, then looks at the items the dwarf was holding.

He makes his way to a counter and places the metal items on top with a loud clash as they all bang against each other. A few pieces of chain mail armor, and a couple of weapons like short swords and rapiers. The changeling looks up at him disappointedly and sneers.

"Is this all you got? What about actual armor?"

"I don't keep my better selling items here," Sidereal snorts back, getting low and in the girl's face. "Sure, lots of people come in from the port, but no one's buying armor and weapons in Alpherg. Ain't practical."

"So all we have to choose from are your simple armor sets and some spare weapons?" Urania asks, a little confused. Never before had she heard an excuse from a blacksmith, but the more she thought about it the more it made sense.

"Take it or leave!" Sidereal replies angrily. "I got other things I want to do today. I ain't gonna risk my neck on giving you something you'll just break while in Alpherg."

He turns to Dawn, who isn't standing with the group but instead looking around outside by the entrance.

"Satyr!" Sidereal calls her over. "Come take a look at these fine weapons. You may need one."

"I'm okay." Dawn smiles back. "I prefer to save my money on things I might want later. Plus, I'm more of a supporter than a fighter."

The dwarf grunts, and unhappily makes his way to a room in the back of his shop. Zua and Urania watch him carefully until he gets out of their view. They exchange looks and then glance through the weapons and armor he had picked out. It wasn't bad, but it wasn't good either. Only slightly better than what they were wearing currently.

"I guess we can take the armor." Zua frowns, pulling out a pouch of gold from her bag.

"It's better than nothing," Urania mimics her almost to perfection.

Sidereal returns and helps the two with their purchases. As the girls don their new armor, he walks up to the satyr in the entryway. He sticks out his hand and drops a blue bladed rapier into her hands. Engraved into the blade itself were runes that seemed to be written in dwarven.

"This is beautiful!" Dawn's eyes glitter, reflecting the radiant hue of the sword. "What do the runes say?"

"Blaze like a star," Sidereal replies and starts walking away.

"Blaze like—"

"Only say those words when you wish to activate its power!" The concern in the blacksmith's voice was a little off putting for the girls. One could say they preferred his grumpy demeanor.

"Oh." Dawn blushes. "Thank you, but I can't afford this."

"It is a gift," Sidereal says, turning his back to her and walking to the counter to sit down. "Think of it as an advance, as a thanks for taking care of Gibbous."

"I can't accept this."

Sidereal glares at the bard, who, under the pressure of the smith, places it around her waist. Zua looks to the dwarf unhappily and places her leather armor on the counter.

"Why does she get a special item? And for free?"

"She didn't complain about my services upon entering my shop." Sidereal doesn't release his scowl when he faces Zua. "It's fine to want to be a hero, but you have too much pride. Anything can happen in battle."

"You say that as though we're going to fail," Urania says, fitting her new armor to her body.

"I do not believe anything is certain until the end of the fight. And I don't like to see warriors enter a battle ill-equipped."

"What if we are ill-equipped for this battle, huh?" Zua stomps stubbornly. Sidereal slides a few gold pieces into the pile that Urania and Zua used to pay for their armor before handing it back to the barbarian.

"You ain't," he replies, dumping the gold into her hands. "You're just being childish right now. Go, or you'll be late."

Muttering under her breath, Zua leads the group out of the forge and north toward the palace. Urania slows down, glancing over her shoulder towards Sidereal's and then at the ground. She picks up her pace again, catching up to the other two as they climb the hill leading to their destination.

◆

At the top of the hill was a wide expansion that seemed to be flattened to make room for the palace. The pavement seemed clean, and the grass was well trimmed, with rows of bushes in the shapes of bears lined up all the way to the entrance. A large fountain with a massive bear, standing in the center, with a crown on its head was placed halfway from the edge of the hill to the building.

"Hey! Over here!" a childish voice calls out to the trio from the fountain and the girls see the boy in blue along with two robed individuals.

"Oh great," Zua moans, slouching over as though she was already beaten.

"What's wrong?" Dawn asks. "Are you sick? Did you tire yourself out climbing the hill."

"No," Zua sighs, hitting her face with her hand, and dragging it down to her chin. "It's nothing."

This explains where that Master Blue guy was then. Figures Comet had to ruin my fun.

The trio makes their way up to the three people standing at the palace's foot. Upon reaching them, they get a closer look at the two others with Comet. They were a man and a young woman, both looking to be half elves with light blue eyes and radiant white hair. The girl has a few braids tying her hair back behind her looking like a crown, while the man has a well-trimmed goatee. Both are in robes the color of sand. and holding a staff in one of their hands with a dragon and crystal on the end.

"Welcome," the man greets them, bowing in a slow respectful manner.

"It is a pleasure to make your acquaintance. I am Master Blue of the Shrine of Draco here in Alpherg, and royal advisor to the late King Ursa Major. This is my apprentice, Cyan."

The man gestures to the woman standing next to him, and she mimics his actions by bowing before the trio. Her gentle smile and kind eyes fall onto Zua for a moment before she speaks.

"Comet has been keeping us up to date on the status of you three. He believes that you will be quite useful in this mission."

"And exactly what is our plan of attack here?" Zua asks, still very annoyed that Comet was responsible for her not being able to see the Shrine of Draco.

"Well." Comet squeezes himself between the two parties. "What I was hoping to do was rush the guards in each room, leaving a member of the Shrine to intercept any backup that may follow."

He twirls his hand in the air, emitting blue streams of sparkles. The streams collide and begin to meld into a holographic image of the palace. Dawn looks in wonder at Comet's magical ability, and then thinks to check his other hand. Sure enough, he was holding onto his pocket watch, which was sticking out of his coat pocket ever so slightly.

"First, Master Blue will create a distraction for the guards out here in the entrance, this should swarm many of them to his position. Next in the Main Hall, Cyan will immobilize any who are stationed directly inside that did not exit the building. Lastly, we will sneak past them into the Dining Hall and the Hall to the Throne taking care of the rest."

"That's quite thought out." Urania nods. Comet smiling happily and standing up a little taller to welcome more praise.

"Yeah, no," Zua said, waving her hand in his illusion. The boy sinks to his knees as he watches his spell dissolve in front of his eyes. Blue chuckles and looks at the changeling.

"What would you have us do then?"

Zua stops to think for a moment, Urania and Dawn looking at her with anticipation. Then the barbarian reaches into her bag and pulls out a sickle. She tosses it around in her hands a bit and smiles menacingly toward the palace.

"You guys have the ability to shapeshift into dragons, don't you?"

Cyan smiles and her eyes look at her master. He laughs nervously and smiles, then nods slowly, not understanding where she was going with her question.

"Well, as I see it," Zua continues, "we have you stay out here in that dragon form and lure all the guards you can out to the entrance, and I'll take care of the rest inside. Then your friend here can hold off anyone behind us."

"That's kind of what I said," Comet whimpers softly to himself, still on the ground looking at the place where his magic was casted.

"Yeah, but," Zua points her sickle in his direction, "I have a little something I've been meaning to try out."

"What is that thing?" Dawn whispers to Urania. The demon responds with a shrug and a confused expression.

She knew Zua was a well-trained bounty hunter before she met her, but she had never seen the changeling with a weapon like that. As a matter of fact, she was certain that Zua didn't have a sickle on her before they met, and never came across one on their journey's together. Unless . . .

"Where did you get that?" Urania shoves Zua's shoulder, pushing her forward a little.

"I had it for a while," Zua says softly, not looking at her friend. "Long before we met. I promise."

"That isn't important now," Cyan speaks up. "We should get moving before the guards get suspicious as to why we're just standing here."

The woman reaches into her robe and pulls out a small pebble, tossing it into the air. After a few seconds of ascending into the air she speaks in a language that neither Urania nor Dawn understood and shot a bolt of lightning from her staff.

"That's the language of dragons!" Zua exclaims.

"For someone who could tell we were dragon druids." Blue laughs. "This is the thing that surprises you. I hope you're prepared to be completely amazed then."

As the lightning hits the pebble, an explosion of white smoke engulfs the majority of the area the group and guards are standing in. Blue then takes a deep breath in and closes his eyes. He drops to all four, beginning to morph and grow into a scaly humanoid creature. Guards by the entrance of the palace start shouting for assistance from inside.

SIEGE ON ALPHERG PALACE

As more troops start rushing out, Comet and Cyan grab the trio and pull them out of the smoky area toward the main entrance to the building. The sound of armor and metal weapons clanging around pass them as about thirty men start running toward their distraction. Out of the smoke comes a roar and a bright shining light.

"That's our cue to head in." Cyan pulls on Urania's arms and starts running toward the entrance of the Main Hall.

"How do you know?" Zua asks, being dragged along by Comet with Dawn right behind them. Her armor, along with Urania's, begin to spark with white crackles.

"If you stay out here." Comet grins. "You'll get your answer, but also be turned into a roasted changeling."

The group reaches the door and steps inside just as the source of the roar emerges out of the cloud of smoke. With a beat of his wings, Blue clears the area. revealing his form to be a giant white-scaled dragon. His eyes are blue like the sky, and teeth and claws are razor sharp. From his mouth, he breathes out a flash of a white lightning bolt that pass through all thirty of the guards in a chain, locking onto each one standing next to each other.

Zua's eyes widen, and her jaw drops to the ground, realizing the immense power that the Draco druids held. A spark of inspiration lights up in her but is followed by the calls of a man across the hall.

"Hey! Who are you?!"

The group turns to look behind them, seeing that over a dozen more armored guards are posted inside with weapons drawn at them. Cyan sighs and steps forward, clenching her staff in her hands. Her eyes flash a bright blue, like lightning streaking across the sky.

"The four of you move on ahead," she says over her shoulder without looking at the group, as a few of the armed guards start approaching her slowly, "these men are outnumbered, but I fear there may be more of them further ahead."

"This might be your chance to show us that thing." Urania winks at Zua before running to a wall to stay clear of Cyan.

"Outnumbered?" One of the guards walking up to the woman laughs. "You must be confused sweetie."

He gets about a foot away from her and reaches out his hand to grab her staff. Then a sharp pain begins to tingle from his wrist up through his arm. He looks down, and in horror, lets out a terrible scream of pain as he sees no hand connected to his arm. A knight that had been beside him had sliced it off and was holding his position.

"What the hell is wrong with you?!" the handless guard shrieks, dropping his weapon to hold his wound.

"Lady Cyan." The guard stands up straight and salutes. "Our infiltration has been a success. Shall we clean up the palace?"

"Let us begin!"

Cyan's voice echoes in the Main Hall, and over half the guards turn to face the others, taking off their helmets to reveal their faces. They were half-elf men and women with blue eyes and white hair, imposter guards set as a trap for this very mission. They began swinging their swords at the real guards, catching them all by surprise. Cyan looks at Comet and nudges her head towards the door before running off to fight herself.

"Let's go!" the boy says, leaping high into the air above the battle that has broken out.

He lands softly beside Urania, who has taken the time to run the length of the wall to the door. Zua huffs and begins to change her form as she proceeds to use claws growing from her fingers to scale a pillar. As she reaches the darkened ceiling, all Dawn is able to catch a glimpse of is a white scaled tail slinking into the shadows.

"Dawn! Hurry!"

The satyr breaks back into reality to see the half-demon calling to her from an opened door across the room. A few quick breaths in, and the girl is racing through the crowd of guards and elves fighting; dodging swinging blades and stray streams of lightning bolts coming from Cyan's staff. A cacophony of yelling and metal clanging nearly deafens her, but she miraculously reaches the others on the opposite side.

Pulling her in, Comet turns back to the door and latches it shut. He turns to face his hired help with a smile that changes to a frown instantaneously.

"Zua? Where's Zua?" Comet counts the heads of the girls only to find two sets of horns and not a small barbarian along with them.

"Never mind that." Dawn points ahead of her. "We got company."

Urania and Comet follow her finger toward the center of the room. Tables with candelabras and plates piled with food are lined up in neat rows, dressed in white lining cloth with red and gold trims. A few plants and portraits decorate the walls with hanging lanterns to light up the darker corners. In the center, between a few rows of the dining tables, were five guards and one very large orc guard in black armor.

"Captain! Intruders!"

"Well," the orc sneers, "this ain't your lucky day. Wandering into the palace uninvited-like is punishable by DEATH!"

A roar leaves his gaping mouth, along with a stream of drool and specs of spit. His voice echoes in the room and invigorates his men who proceed to run towards the group. Dawn cowers, guarding her face with her arms, while Comet and Urania step in front of her ready to meet the fight.

Then, as if a response to the orc's mighty bellow, a hissing snarl comes from the ceiling. The guards stop in their tracks just a few feet away from their intended targets and look up. From the darkness, a figure cloaked in shadow drops down. Small bat-like wings spread out to a five-foot span, and a white scaly tail beats the ground. Sharp pointed teeth grin and the creature's blue reptilian eyes peer down its snout at the fear struck men. A shadow of menace engulfs the human-sized armored white dragon as it pulls a large sickle glowing with runes burning like fire from behind its back.

"Monster!"

"Demon!"

"Run!"

The guards scramble backward, dropping their weapons and racing toward the door behind them. The orc guard takes a step back, squinting at the creature in front of him. It WAS a white dragon, but it was small and even more standing perfectly upright like a human.

The dragon begins to laugh hysterically and turns to the three heroes behind it.

"Did you see the looks on their faces?"

The dragon's skin begins to melt and morph into a more humanoid shape. Scales and horns dissolve into long brown hair and skin, its claws and sharp teeth to nails and proud grin of the lost barbarian Zua.

"What the heck?" Urania runs up to her friend and hugs her tightly. "That was so cool, how come you've never done that before?"

"I only just saw a dragon today thanks to that Blue guy."

"But you're a changeling," Dawn mutters to herself, "you shouldn't be able to do that."

"She can though."

Dawn turns to look up at Comet, who was holding his watch tightly in his hand. A serious expression is on his face, but it turns into a soft smile.

"Zua is a special kind of changeling. One could say she's one of a kind. Almost anything she can see, she can turn into that creature no matter the size or body type. However, she does have her limits. It'd be careless to think that she's invincible."

Dawn looks at Urania and Zua who were laughing and smiling. She felt a strange curiosity begin to brew in her. What other amazing people were there in this world, and do they have awesome powers like Zua's? The bard's thoughts are interrupted by a loud snort from the center of the room.

"You're petty tricks ain't gonna work on me! I ain't scared of no half-pint!"

The orc guard draws his weapon, a large black scimitar with sharp-edged teeth along the blade. Zua looks over to him with disappointment and sighs. The orc walks forward, slowly, unsure of his next move or his opponents, but only one thing was in his mind.

"I WILL KILL YOU!"

The massive guard raises the blade over his head and brings it down to the floor, forcing the half-demon and changeling to leap back in order to dodge. The scimitar wedges itself into the floor and the orc tries to pull it free. The four heroes back up against the door leading to the Main Hall, feeling someone trying to push it open.

"Crap!" Dawn yelps, pushing against the door with her body, trying to keep it closed. "They're trying to get in!"

"Guys," Zua says, nudging Comet in the side, "on my mark run to the other side of the room."

"But the guard," Comet protests, "Urania and Dawn won't be able to get past him."

"I'll make an opening! Just trust me!"

Urania nods and grabs Dawn by the hand. Comet groans and clicks his watch, disappearing instantly and reappearing by the door leading to the Hall to the Throne. A worried look comes over his face as he slips through the door.

"Now!" Zua rushes toward one of the dining tables and lifts it up. It is much lighter than the one in the goblin settlement, and she swings it into the orc, pressing him into one of the walls with portraits.

Seeing the chance, Urania pulls Dawn along, both racing towards the door and sliding through with no problem. Zua takes a moment to catch her breath and then follows her friends. As she steps forward, reaching for the door, the room turns pitch black, and all the walls disappear.

The barbarian looks around and sees nothing but absolute darkness, even beneath her feet was a sheet of shadow with no reflection. Instinctively, she turns around and grabs her sickle, feeling an ominous presence around her.

"Zua . . . Apis . . ."

"Who's there?" The barbarian calls out into the darkness, but there is no reply. Then a figure slowly approaches her from out of nowhere.

The form was that of a person, very tall and built like a warrior clad in armor. But the face was either under a helmet or didn't exist at all because the figure has no eyes, mouth, or any facial features. To top it all off, it was glowing red like it was on fire, and as it got closer Zua saw that it *was* on fire.

"You're . . . not . . . worthy."

"What?" Zua's face scrunches up in confusion. "What are you talking about?"

"His . . . power," the figure continues to speak, "You're not . . . WORTHY!"

The figure draws a weapon from its side and raises it above its head. It was a sickle, similar to Zua's, but burning like a torch. As the weapon falls down onto her, Zua's eyes shift back to reality. The orc guard was still able to fight and was in front of her with his blade over his head!

With no time to process, Zua feels the scimitar slash her shoulder. Trying to dodge backward, she bumps into the door. A sharp pain is coming from her arm, and as she looks down, shock comes over her. Blood streaming down like a river was coming from the wound. It wasn't bad, but it definitely hurt.

"You're puny tricks," the orc snarled with rage, "will not work on me!"

You are not worthy . . . You will die on the battlefield . . . with no glory.

Words echo in Zua's mind, words of the figure she witnessed. Then, like a fire being lit in her, the barbarian let out a mighty yell, lifting her sickle with one hand and charging at the orc. She slashes at his torso, cutting deeply into his skin. The guard yells in pain but manages to swing his blade into Zua's side. It hurt so much worse than her arm, but she didn't care. All she could hear was . . .

YOU'RE NOT WORTHY!

"Don't fucking talk down to ME!"

The scream is followed by a painful push of adrenaline, as the changeling grabs her weapon with two hands and lifts it up above her head. Blood spurts from her wounds as she puts all her strength into one more attack.

"And you!" Her eyes seething with rage as the orc looms over her. "Stay down this time!"

With a swipe, the blade makes contact with his neck and travels straight through with little resistance. Both stand still for a moment, before the orc guard falls to the side and his head rolls off his body. Zua stands up, dropping her sickle to the ground. She spits at the guards corpse and dislodges the scimitar from her side.

"Not worthy, my ass."

She picks her weapon up again and puts it on her back, stumbling toward the entrance to the Hall to the Throne.

CHAPTER 5

Tyrant King Gibbous

Zua walks into the Hall to the Throne, grabbing her side now seeping with blood from her wound. Further down the hall were two unconscious guards laying on the ground, and past them is Comet, Dawn, and Urania, all talking just a few feet in front of the throne room's entrance. The satyr turns to see the changeling slowly making her way to them and notices her injury.

"Zua!" Dawn cries out, racing toward her friend. "What happened? We were worried about you."

"It's nothing," the barbarian replies, using her other hand to feel the sickle strapped to her back, "just had to finish that big guard off so he wouldn't follow us."

She couldn't bring herself to explain exactly what truly happened to her. The vision and the voice might sound like she was trying to pull their legs. She wasn't lying though about having to fight the guard, and as she figured it, he would have followed them to the throne room anyway.

"I advise that we still try not to kill anyone," Comet sighs, putting a hand on his forehead and shaking it, "after all these men are probably all under Gibbous's charm magic."

The girls nod with a moan, because if Comet was right on his guess, it would make the guards mostly innocent for everything they've been putting people through over the last six months. The boy reaches into his pocket and pulls out his pocket watch, clicking it out. A bright blue light pulsates from the face while Comet looks down at it before closing it again.

"The time has come." He smiles from ear to ear. "And we can finally get on with our true mission too!"

"True mission?" Zua grumbles. Comet had been way too secretive about what he had hired them for and Zua, for one, was having enough of it.

"Don't worry." Comet raises his hands up, hoping to reassure the changeling. "Once we are done dealing with this tyrant king, I'll explain everything in full detail."

"Well, you might have to repeat it later then." Dawn twirls one of her curls of hair around her horn. She is looking down at the ground and using the toe of her hoof to draw circles on the floor.

"Because Urania left while you weren't looking."

Comet raises a finger and starts counting the heads in front of him. One. Two. Three? Wait! Where was the third?! He knew for certain that Urania was standing next to him when Zua came in and when he was checking his watch. So where could she have possibly gone in such a short period of time?

"I need to think about getting her a bell." Comet covers his face with his hands then pulls them back into his hair.

"You should have known that bringing a bounty hunter thief into a palace was going to end up like this."

Zua's smirk antagonizes Comet who looks dismissively at her. With a small stomp and a huff, the boy straightens out his tail coat and turns to face the door.

"We continue the plan. With or without a full group."

Using both of his hands, he pushes the great doors of the throne room open. Inside is a lavishly decorated area with marble statue pillars supporting the ceiling. On the walls are portraits of the great kings of Alpherg, all of them large bears with a crown on their head and a scepter in hand, or paw to be more accurate. In between each are a suit of armor, golden with red accents, each holding a unique weapon from axes to halberds. In the center is a long red carpet with gold trim on the border leading up a small staired stage where a massive wooden throne lies.

The seat of the king of Alpherg is made of rich dark oak, with bear faces and claws painted in red and gold. A sculpted bear head wearing a crown is centered at the top of the throne with the paws at the ends of the arms. On either side stands two guards in armor, with their swords drawn and standing vertically in front of them with their hands on top. The magnificent sight is easily overlooked by the grotesque creature sitting in its beauty.

A large and stout man, wearing only his white undergarments and a thick silk red cape, is lounging on the throne, spread out in a sloppy manner as though he was lying in bed. He picks his nose with his finger, pulls it out, and examines it before flicking the contents at a guard standing post. The man laughs and scratches his bulbous gut, turning to see the trio of uninvited guests. He sits up a little bit, and pulls on his unkempt white beard, peering at the approaching group.

"Who are these guys?!" the man screams in an unsettling high pitched voice.

Concern was definitely in it, but something told Dawn that it was also his natural range, which meant talking to him was going to be an experience her ears would never recover from.

"Gibbous." Comet raises his hands into the air as though he was greeting the man as an old friend. "What a surprise it is to see you hear."

"Same could be said about you, Comet," Gibbous snaps back, sitting up straight and inching as far back into the throne as he could.

"Last I heard, you left Sol six months ago. When did you come back?"

"I was out looking for some people that could help me," the boy replies, gesturing to Dawn and Zua behind him. "And I've been in town for a little while now. Probably no more than a week or two."

Gibbous snorts, moving his hand slowly to grab something from behind the seat while still facing forward.

"I see. Well, as you know, I am king now of the beautiful Alpherg. Some may say I'm suited for this position. It's quite an honor."

"Suited for it?" Zua steps forward. "Are you living in a fantasy or something? You have been nothing but a nuisance for us since we got here."

"Not to mention how you've treated the lower class people and most importantly the goblins." Dawn inserts herself in the conversation as well.

"The goblins?" Gibbous stops his searching and squints at the satyr. "I did get word that my men failed at the settlement of those green monsters, and that three people fought alongside them. Are you telling me it was you?"

"What do you have against the goblins?" Comet asks. "They have been a good help to Alpherg in fending off monsters from Carina Forest along with partaking in commerce and trade. Oort is a strong and good leader who poses no threat to the city or to you. So why are you targeting them?"

The untidy man stands up and begins pacing around the throne.

"The goblins are a menace! If left unchecked they could turn on us at any time! Their kind have proven to be savage creatures, killing and raping civilians all for the sake of just because!"

"These are rumors and actions of the past." Comet points at the man, now making his way behind the throne.

"Everyone knows that they have changed their ways. And for the last century there have been no acts of aggression from them or ill-mannered deeds."

Gibbous appears on the other side of the great chair, now holding a black scepter with a small pink orb on the top. He starts hitting the orb on his palm while looking at the ground, making his way in front of his seat again.

"Maybe so, but it could all be a ploy, to give a sense of false security. Lying to the good people of Alpherg and Sol!"

"Like you are doing currently?" Comet smirks. Gibbous sweats and takes a step back.

"What are you talking about?"

"I know for certainty that King Ursa Major was healthy and in good spirits when I left Sol six months ago. And if something unfortunate did end up happening to him, he had a son who was ready to take the throne after him. So, I say again, what a surprise to see you hear."

Zua and Dawn exchange a look of guilty pleasure and a smile, knowing that Comet has laid his trap out on the floor and was now just waiting for Gibbous to entangle himself in it.

"No!" Gibbous's face starts turning a shade of red and his eyes squint and water. "I am king. I was given the position fair and square by the guards of the palace. They lost faith in the royal family and thought that I should be in charge."

"That's not a very legitimate way of becoming the ruler of a city." Comet quickly strikes down the man's argument.

"Not to mention, you have no experience or credentials for such a position."

The man's face grows redder, and his beard starts to frizz up. Comet raises up his pointer finger and smiles victoriously, accompanying it with a giggle. He was looking down at the floor and reaching into his pocket with his other hand.

"There's one more thing I just couldn't figure out until I saw it today in the goblin settlement. Dawn, how does charm magic work?"

The satyr cocks her head to the side and thinks on the question. After a little bit of time, she comes up with her answer.

"The user is able to control the minds of those around them as long as they are within the presence of those they wish to charm. Also, it normally only works on creatures of the same type, so charming animals and creatures is normally difficult."

"In the goblin settlement, the men you sent were all still under your spell, and not to mention you had a warg who seemed to be very well trained compared to their normal vicious nature." Comet's eyes look up to the king, glowing bright blue with sparkles like the universe was captured in them.

"You have made a deal with a Yokubo, a Dream Demon! You have extended the power of your magic to overthrow the old king and take the throne for your own personal pleasure. That said, this was all possible thanks to that Wishing Star you have there."

Comet points toward the scepter, and Gibbous's face burns bright red. The pink orb on the scepter glows bright as well and Gibbous points it at the two guards standing post.

"You know something, Comet?! I've had enough people looking down on me! I'm putting an end to my misery and suffering! I'm taking control of my future!"

"By stealing the lives of others? What are they doing to you that is so bad?" Dawn stomps her hoof into the floor.

"Those goblins know too much! Plus, they are a sore sight in my beautiful city! They don't deserve to be a part of it!" Gibbous squeals and blasts a ray of pink sparkles into the faces of the guards.

"What a pig!" Zua gets into a battle stance. "This guy thinks he's so high and mighty, but he's nothing more than a whiny man child."

"I have given you chance after chance," Comet says softly, clenching his fists. "But you never seemed to want to make an actual change. Now you resort to dark forces and cheap tricks that are affecting people's lives, all so you can live royally?"

"Damn you all! Men! KILL THEM! Treasonous lowlife scum shouldn't dirty my palace!"

"You're right." Comet points to the tyrant. "Girls! Let's clean this palace of the fat bastard's reign!"

◆

Urania walks toward a door to the left of the group, while Comet is talking, leading into a long hallway with red walls and lush red carpeting. Some plants and portraits decorate the area as though it were a museum instead of a castle. Embedded on the walls are a series of doors, leading to a few random rooms, which, by her guess, seemed to be living quarters for servants. Entering one of them, the half-demon is greeted by a few suits of armor that the guards of the palace were wearing.

"I guess this wouldn't hurt," she says to herself, grabbing a helmet and robe with the colors of the Alpherg guards.

"Might even make sneaking around here a bit easier."

After properly adorning her accessories, she sticks her head out of the doorway to make sure no one was passing by. The hallway seemed unusually empty for a palace, but with no one around, there was no one to get into trouble with. She steps out of the room and continues down, away from the Hall to the Throne.

At the end of the stretch, the hallway comes up onto a fork going left and right. Urania looks down both ways to figure out which would probably be better for her. She wasn't looking for anything in particular, but she didn't want to run into anyone who might recognize her as not an actual guard.

The left way has a few guards posted around a room with a few of them exiting and entering it. If she had to guess, that was going to be the barracks or at least a lounge area for the guards. To the right, however, it seems as though a few maids were going in and out of the rooms, holding baskets of what appear to be laundry. Upon further inspection, the furthest room seemed different from all the others, looking a bit more luxurious.

"Oh!" Urania grins mischievously, slowly making her way to the end of the right hall.

She quietly comes up to an open door and peers into the room. A maid with a black dress and white lace headpiece was hunched over a bed and tucking a sheet into the sides of a mattress. Her short orange hair bobbed with her slight motions, but her back remained to the door. Grabbing her spaded tail, the half-demon tiptoes past the doorway and hugs up against the wall on the other side. A sigh of relief escapes her, and she turns toward her main goal.

In front of her is a room with a double door entrance made of red wood and gold decorations. The frame is white and has small bears carved from the bottom to the top. The doorknobs themselves resembled bear heads with small ruby-like jeweled eyes.

"Either Gibbous has a thing for bears or the previous king was some kind of animal," Urania grumbles, quite tired of all the seemingly connected decor.

She reaches for the door handle and turns it slowly. A small click unlatches the two tall pieces of wood, and she looks over her shoulder while pushing the door open with a soft creak. Inside is dark due to a window being draped with a dark colored curtain, but some sunlight was making its way through. Leaving the door open enough to give herself a little light to see with, Urania walks in and starts to look around.

A giant framed painting of a half-naked man with a large belly almost takes up an entire wall. He is wearing nothing but a lush red cape and white underwear, and on his head seems to be a makeshift crown made out of paper.

"Oh gods." Urania feels the taste of vomit fill her mouth, but manages to hold it back. "This guy really is a bitch."

Across from the artistic ego is a large bed with a red canopy over it. Gold trim and tassels add a little more color to it and make it seem proper and neat. The bed itself is a complete contrast, having three pillows laying in the center with a bed sheet half folded and laying on the ground.

"He's childish too. I bet this guy would be powerless if he didn't have all those guards."

Urania turns her attention away from the bed for now and walks over to the side of it, where a large dresser made of oak lined with gold fastenings and handles sits. On top of it are what appear to be magical notes on the components for a special potion that makes people follow your every command, along with a bottle half filled with a pink liquid. Next to it is a folded piece of paper, and curious about its contents, Urania picks it up and reads it aloud to herself quietly.

"Great Dream Demon, I have done as you have asked of me. I have located the other Wishing Stars and have marked them on the map you gave to me. As part of our deal, I ask that you give me absolute power over the people of Alpherg and help me rid the city of the goblins so that I can rule without any resistance."

Urania folds the paper and puts it back on the dresser next to the bottle.

"Wait a second!"

The half-demon grabs the bottle quickly and holds it up to the light coming from the hallway. It is empty except for a few drops down at the base. But it had more than that in there. She was sure of it. Her eyes dart across the room, checking to see if anyone was with her. She didn't see anyone or anything.

"Odd." She scratches her chin and starts opening up the dresser drawers and rummaging through them.

"I better find that map he wrote about quickly. Might be useful later. Plus, these Wishing Star things sound like they are important, and important things fetch a good price."

A smirk streaks across her face as she thinks about the riches she could have. She continues to search through underwear and clothes that seem to be dirty, sweaty, and stink of body odor even though they are put into a place for clean laundry. One of the briefs was stained and crusted, and Urania felt the feeling of vomiting return. She drops the clothes into the drawer and steps back, covering her mouth.

"I swear! This man is a real pain!" Her tail shivers out of disgust and falls limp to the ground, as though it, too, could smell the putrid stench of the man's unwashed clothing.

"Excuse me," a soft voice from the doorway breaks Urania's dramatic moment, "what are you doing here?"

The half-demon slowly turns her head to the entrance of the room, and standing in the doorway is the orange haired maid from the other room holding a basket of bed sheets. Her green eyes glistened, and a look of fear was washing over her face. She seemed frightened by the sight of Urania and was holding the door in front of her as protection.

"I, uh, work here?" Urania stumbles a sentence out of her mouth. Immediately she smacks herself in the face with her hand, making the maid ease up from her tension and giggle.

"I mean," the maid continues, now smiling softly, "I figured that. What I meant was what are you doing in the king's quarters?"

Urania thought quickly, searching the room for a lie that she could use. Wait, maybe she didn't need a full one, just a half of a lie would work in this situation. For all the maid knew, she was a guard; after all she was dressed just like one. She opens her mouth and lays out her best chance to get what she was looking for.

"The king sent me to his quarters, these quarters, to look for a map he had made up. He wanted to review it before he gave it to the Dream Demon."

"Dream Demon?" The maid's face returns to a state of surprise and horror. Maybe Urania told a little too much of the truth with that one.

"Yes?" She felt like she was grabbing at strings that were leading to nowhere. "But he said it wasn't bad. He just wanted to look at it again."

The maid looks down, seemingly not convinced by the half-demon. Urania glances at her hand to see her clench the door, maybe still afraid. She wasn't looking at her anymore and might run to the other guards for help or worse to have them attack her, which would absolutely ruin her plans of finding that map. Urania takes a slow and deep breath in, reaching down towards her dagger with a snails movement. She didn't want to frighten the girl anymore, but if she left it was over.

"I think I understand." The maid stands up straight and does not lift her head to look at the half-demon. Urania could hear her heartbeat in her ear.

Please. Don't run. Just be calm.

"That paper you're looking for is on the bed. I saw Gibbous try to hide it there this morning."

With a gentle smile, the maid lifts her head to Urania. Tears are streaming down her cheeks, but her emerald eyes are filled with relief. She winks to the half-demon and starts to close the door.

"I'll wait out here until you're done."

As the door closes, Urania hunches over and gasps for air as though she had been pushed down under water for the whole interaction. After recovering herself, she walks over to the bed and moves one of the canopy's curtains aside. Lifting up one of the pillows, a feeling of victory comes over her as a neatly folded scrap of paper lies on the bed.

Picking it up and unraveling it, the rogue studies its contents. A map of the whole continent of Sol was drawn on it with nine star markings all over it. Four have words written next to them: Polaris, Sirius, Bellatrix, and Regulus. Not sure what to do, Urania comes up with the idea to make a duplicate copy for herself. She turns and bends down to the ground, pulling off her bag to look for a piece of paper. Finally finding one, she turns back to the bed, only to find the pillows.

"What the . . ." are the only words she is able to mutter when the door opens again.

She turns to look at what is happening, pulling her dagger out in the process. It was just the maid, except she looked a little worried now. She is closing the door and trying to push it with her body when a guard slips in through the opening.

Urania instinctively lunges toward him with her blade going to stab him in the side. The guard, with little movement, grabs her wrist, twists, and bends her arm behind her back. Wincing at the minor pain, Urania tries to look over her shoulder at the man, getting a glimpse of his eyes behind the helmet.

Blue and reptilian.

"Sorry, ma'am." The guard turns to the maid. "The new rookie here was just following orders to make sure no imposters get into the king's room."

The maid looks confusedly at the man as he begins to escort Urania out of the hall and back toward the Hall of the Throne. She doesn't do anything to try and stop the man but grabs her basket and timidly walks back into the room, closing the door behind her.

"Are you who I think you are?" Urania whispers as the guard lets go of her and starts leading her down the corridor.

"I think my question far outranks yours." The guard takes off his helmet and reveals his longer white hair, deep blue eyes, and slightly pointed ears. He was one of the members of Master Blue's group that infiltrated the palace as an imposter.

"Why are you exploring while the others made it to Gibbous?"

"I may have found something important." Urania smiles happily. "Gibbous is looking for something valuable and I know where to find some of them."

The half elf chuckles to himself, walking swiftly down to the entrance of the Hall to the Throne. His expression was all that Urania needed to know that she had stumbled onto something big.

"This is part of my group's mission, isn't it?"

Excitement fills her spirit as the two of them enter the hallway before the throne room. Loud yelling and clanging was coming from behind the doors. The half-demon takes a deep breath and grabs both of her dagger and busts through the door to join her friends in battle.

✦

The two guards standing next to Gibbous begin walking down towards Comet, Dawn, and Zua, one grabbing a halberd from one of the suits of armor, while the other a sword. Comet pulls out his watch from his pocket and presses down on the button on the side. Instantaneously, everything around him stops, Gibbous in mid scream, the guards caught in their stride, even Dawn and Zua preparing to charge into battle.

Taking a few steps in front of him, Comet slides past the guards and walks up to Gibbous. His watch's face begins to flash blue, and he responds by pressing the button again. As he does, everyone returns to their actions as though nothing had happened. Only now, Gibbous was staring the boy face to face, and Comet's darkened face and angry eyes brought him nothing but instant terror.

"WAAAHHH!!!" Tears build in the stout man's eyes, as he waves his scepter in front of him as if he were scaring off a wild animal.

"Gibbous," Comet sighs deeply, "you poor unfortunate soul. What has brought you to this? And which Yokubo gave you the Wishing Star?"

"Wishing Star?" Dawn perks up at the mention of the mysterious item again.

"Heads up!"

Zua races in front of her and blocks the halberd strike with her sickle. Dawn steps aside as Zua is brought to her knee still trying to hold her block. The satyr turns her head to notice the second guard approaching with his sword above his head and aiming at Zua.

"Not gonna happen!"

She lowers her head, appearing like a ram and kicks her leg behind her like a bull. With a stomp, she charges at the man and collides her horns with his stomach, tossing him a few feet back and into one of the suits of armor along the wall.

"Don't kill them!" Comet calls over his shoulder, making sure that the girls hear him. "They are just under Gibbous's control, so they may not actually be our enemies."

Gibbous grins maliciously, seeing his attack of opportunity. He lifts his scepter and brings it down on the back of Comet's head. Letting out a victorious laugh, saliva sticks to his beard, and he rubs it off his face before calling out.

"How do you like that?! Guess I didn't need that silly star or the Dream Demon to beat you, did I?!"

A small tap on his shoulder sends chills to rush up the tyrant's spine. He spins around to see the boy in blue standing behind him, completely fine.

"Dream Demon, you say? So, you *are* working with a Yokubo, like I thought!"

"But how?"

Gibbous was certain he got a hit on the boy. He looks down at the ground where Comet should have been lying. Instead, he found one of the suits of armor in a pile, the helmet having a large dent in the back of it. Facing Comet again, the false king begins stepping backward before making a run for the exit.

Zua's arm was growing tired, but the force of the guard wasn't giving up. She had the disadvantage from not just being on the ground but being underneath the attack as well. She puffs up her chest and feels a rage build inside of her, breaking away and moving to the side. The halberd slams into the ground, embedding itself into the floor.

"I got you now!" Zua's fiery eyes smile as she leaps at the guard, her sickle overhead. Just as she was about to strike, a pain rings in her head, burning like a hot coal.

You're not worthy!

Distracted by the voice, the changeling misses her chance, and the guard retaliates with a backhand, pushing her behind him. As she hits the guards, she sees the stumpy feet of Gibbous racing past her. She reaches to catch his ankle but falls short, feeling another sharp pain, but this time in her side. The guard had turned around and stabbed her with the pointed end of his weapon.

Dawn, witnessing everything, thinks to catch the tyrant off guard with her magic. She raises her hand and turns her eyes away. A small light starts emitting from her palm, growing larger at a rapid rate.

"Sensory Flare!"

Dawn's words echo in the room and a brilliant white light fills the area like a small sun in her hand. Being only a few feet away from Gibbous, the flash startles him and makes him fall backwards. After a few seconds, the light fades and the bard turns back around to see that she managed to stop him!

"I did it!"

"Not for long! Eldritch Blast!" the stout man growls lifting his scepter.

The satyr's celebration is cut short as an inky black void appears in front of her. From the void a collection of black tendrils swarm out and begin to lash at her. Bracing herself to be hit, the bard lifts her arms over her head and closes her eyes. The sound of tendrils hitting something and a cry of pain follow, but she remains unharmed. Opening her eyes again, Dawn sees Comet with his back to Gibbous, protecting her.

"You fool!" Gibbous laughs as the magical attack subsides. He stands up and begins running toward the door. Dawn goes to reach for him but sees Comet falling from the hit and goes to catch him instead.

From the boy's hand, Dawn sees the glint of blue from his watch between his fingers. Moving it to get a better look, she notices that the face of the watch was instead replaced with a map of Sol, with twelve white dots flashing on it. Where Alpherg was, two dots were flashing.

"Guess the cat's out of the bag." Comet chuckles weakly.

"What is this?" Dawn couldn't find anything else to say.

Her question is immediately interrupted by the sound of Zua crying out in pain. Looking in the direction of the noise, she is reminded of her comrade being on the ground with the guard stabbing her overhead.

"Go help her. I'll get Gibbous," Comet says softly, trying to lift himself up to his feet. He takes a few steps forward and falls, Dawn catching him.

"I can't."

The bard felt a stinging pain in her heart. Comet and Zua needed her help, and she was the only one who could stop Gibbous from escaping. But she couldn't do all three. Tears were building in her eyes.

Mom . . . Dad . . . What should I do?

Gibbous's laugh echoes in the room as he reaches for the handle of the door.

"Sorry, I'm late! I got distracted."

Long black hair paired with blue spiral horns enter the room. Urania's words brought an air of relief to the entire group, as she slams the door open in Gibbous' face.

"Why you! How did you break free from my control?" Gibbous steps back, clenching his scepter. He waves his hand over the pink crystal and pulls from it a mist of pink dust shimmering with sparkles. He throws it in Urania's face, and she reels backward.

"No!" Zua screams, finding her strength again, now burning in her blood.

She grabs the end of the halberd and breaks it in half. The guard steps backward and watches the changeling shift her face into its natural form. Pitch black eyes and pale white skin. Her hair became frayed, and silver and her nails grew to resemble claws. The guard lets out a yelp of terror before falling to the floor. Zua starts taking slow, painful steps toward her friend in the doorway.

"You're too late!" The tyrant laughs. "She's under my control and there's nothing you can—"

"ACHOO!"

Urania lets out a huge sneeze, sending the magical dust back into Gibbous's face. The man, bewildered, looks the girl up and down a few times before shrieking. She was completely fine, and no trace of his influence was over her.

"You fool." A chuckle breaks out behind him. He turns to find Dawn walking toward him, with Comet leaning on her for support. The bard's smile was full of pride with a hint of vice, the first anyone in the room had seen.

"Don't you know if a person knows you're trying to use charm magic on them, it won't work. That's basic magic knowledge."

Gibbous begins to walk backward away from Dawn and Comet along with the exit where Urania was approaching him from. He feels a hand place itself on his shoulder. Turning his head to look, he sees the true face of Zua, slowly shifting back into that of a human's. Letting out another terrified scream, Gibbous steps forward, finding himself caught in the center of the group.

"You have nowhere to go, and no one to call to for aid." Comet barely is able to make out his words, but powers through it with an intense stare that freezes the tyrant king in place.

"Give up, Gibbous."

"Give up?" The stout man looks down at the ground. It was true. He had nowhere he could run to now and no one left by his side. His eyes flash wide and an evil smirk spreads across his face.

"I'm not done yet, but you are!"

He raises his scepter into the air. The pink orb catches a glint of sunlight coming in from the windows and reflects on a pink hue onto one of the walls. Being partially transparent, the light is able to pass through the gem and reveals a small object encased by the stone—a four-pointed star shape.

"The Wishing Star!" Comet gasps, clenching his side and falling to the floor. His wounds felt like they were burning still, meaning he was in no condition to try and use his abilities.

Damn it. What do we do?

"Great Dream Demon! I ask that you hear me!" Gibbous was now full of glee while a surge of force began to grow around him.

"I wish for the power to defeat these usurpers and claim victory in my battle! Grant me my wish!"

A pink energy starts to swirl from the scepter and down towards his arm. Upon contact, the energy fades into a black color and sounds of hissing and wailing come from the scepter. The gem cracks and the star shaped object breaks free. It sparkles like a diamond in the sunlight, floating in midair as the black energy surrounds it. The shine starts to be consumed by a pitch black smoke inside of the jewel, spreading from the center to the points of the star. Gibbous's maniacal laughter is accompanied by the sound of a vortex of black energy spinning around him.

"Dragon's Lightning!"

From the doorway, a bolt of light flashes, followed by a boom and line of electricity. It weaves its way around Urania and collides with the king. Gibbous cries out in pain, dropping the scepter. It falls into the hand of a tall man, with long white hair and blue eyes, cloaked in sandy robes.

"Master Blue!"

The unison relief of the three girls echoes, as the spiral of wind force slowly fades to nothing, leaving the man at the center lying on the ground with tears in his eyes. The doors burst open even wider, funneling in a large group of robed individuals along with Cyan. She walks up to Comet to help heal him, but he waves her off and points to Zua instead.

Feeling the adrenaline leaving her, Zua collapses to the ground. Both Urania and Cyan run up to her, checking to make sure that she is still breathing. Cyan rolls up the sleeves of her robe and hovers her hands over Zua's wounded side. A soft green glow radiates from the stab wound as Cyan begins to chant softly. Slowly the hole closes, with fibers of flesh and muscle growing at a rapid pace. Zua giggles at the feeling and looks up at Urania.

"That was fun. We should do this more often."

EPILOGUE

The sound of metal shackles being placed on Gibbous's wrists brings an air of relief for Comet as he watches the members of the Shrine of Draco interrogate the man. He shifts his gaze over to Dawn, Urania, and Zua; who is back on her feet after being healed. All of them are excitedly talking to each other, and then the satyr and changeling start scolding the half-demon probably for leaving the group to go exploring. Urania laughs nervously and tries to fend them off by raising her hands to protect her face from Zua's playful punches. A smile breaks across the boy's face.

"You seem happy with the outcome." Blue walks up to Comet, bowing in front of him before continuing his conversation.

"Who wouldn't be?" Comet grins innocently. "My hunch was right, Gibbous had a star. And my second suspicion of him having aid is also spot on."

"Oh?" The tall man looks at him with surprise. "Do you think it is the same person that stole the stars?"

Comet looks down at his hand. In his palm is the crystal star from the tyrant's scepter. A small trace of black impurity lingers inside of it, but its beauty still found a way to break through. Comet could see his reflection, a somber face looking back at him from the edged creases of the object.

"He said it was a Dream Demon, one of the Yokubo."

Blue's expression fell to the floor, his hands folding in front of him. His concern was warranted though. But now was not the time to worry about that. He raises a hand and places it on the boy's shoulder. Comet's eyes catch his, and they exchange a look of content. Right now, the mission was a success, and Alpherg was on the road to fixing the damage of the selfish usurper king. Comet looks back to the girls and takes a deep breath, walking straight for them.

"You can't just run off like that!" Dawn puffs her cheeks at Urania, stomping her hooves onto the floor.

"I'm sorry, I'm sorry. Please, forgive me." Urania laughs while both the bard and Zua stare at her with looks that could burn holes straight through her.

"Where were you anyway?" Zua grumbles.

"Yes," Comet breaks in, stepping into the small circle the group has made, "where were you this whole time? I'd very much like to know myself."

The girls turn to see the boy that hired them limp beside them. In his hand, he was holding the star from Gibbous's scepter instead of his normal pocket watch. A thought breaks into Dawn's mind as she remembers looking at the watch from earlier.

"I was . . ." Urania thinks of something witty to say back to Comet but remembers the map she barely got a glimpse of.

"Actually," Zua interrupts, "you got some explaining to do. I want to know what this whole thing was really about. Are the goblins going to be okay? And what's a Wishing Star?"

Comet smiles and lifts his hand up, holding the star between his finger and thumb.

"Let's start off with the easy one. This is a Wishing Star. Inside of it is a powerful magic energy that grants its holder any wish they possibly can think of with no consequence. It is one of twelve that my people protect in order to bring mortals inspiration."

The three's eyes glow with wonder. An item that powerful was only a few inches away from them, and even more there were twelve of them. Comet reaches into his pocket and pulls out his pocket watch. Flipping it over, he reveals the back of the watch to have a gem exactly like the one he was holding. The only difference was that the one on his watch had a symbol in the center, the sign of the constellation Libra.

"I am in charge of maintaining balance in the World of Wishes. Therefore, I have been given the Wish of Balance. The one we found today is known as the Wish of the Crab. And of course, the goblins will be alright."

126

The girls break back into reality and sigh out of relief.

"Gibbous was the only one who didn't like them." Blue steps into the group's circle and continues Comet's thought.

"He influenced people to segregate them when he gained power, and most people feared that he could get rid of them if they didn't listen to him. However, it seems that Gibbous himself had no real power and just wanted the attention he thought he rightfully deserved. The real danger is the Yokubo that supported him."

"What's a Yokubo?" Zua asks, tilting her head to the side.

"That's the Dream Demon he was referring to when he was trying to use the Wishing Star." Comet looks to the ground somberly before smiling gently at the girls again.

"They are Nashi, creatures of darkness that are opposites to the Sozo like Comet."

"But I thought Comet's race was Negai." Urania scratches her head confusedly.

"The Sozo and Nashi are a collection of eight races," Blue continues, smiling softly as he relays the information to the group.

"The Sozo comprise of the wish-granting, Negai, the dream people, Somni, the emotion spirits, Kanjo, and the lights of hope, Kibo. While the Nashi are their dark counterparts, the demons of desire, Yokubo, the bringers of terror, Akuma, the fog of bleakness, Utsu, and the agents of despair, Raku'tan."

"Someone knows his stuff." Comet humbly smiles at the half-elf.

"It's my duty to aid the king, and knowing about the Sozo and Nashi was one of his wishes."

Blue's smile gives everyone a sense of security and hope. Urania shakes her head, bringing herself back to the earlier conversation.

"I forgot to say I saw Gibbous had a note in his chamber with a map that had markings on it with mention of the Dream Demon."

"Did it specify which one?" Blue steps forward assertively, hoping that the group had a lead to the culprit.

"No, it didn't. Just said Dream Demon." Urania slouches, feeling as though she failed. She feels Zua jab her with her elbow in the side.

She looks down to her changeling friend who was smiling and giving her a thumbs up, trying to help her.

"Nonetheless," Comet says, "this map may be something of interest. Where is it now?"

"On his bed." Urania stands up straight again. "I sort of got interrupted when trying to duplicate it. But I remember the markings and labels. Four places specifically. Regulus, Sirius, Polaris, and Bellatrix."

"Bellatrix?" Dawn feels a shiver crawl up her spine, as she softly repeats the city's name to herself.

"This aligns with your information, Comet." Blue turns to the boy who flips open his pocket watch and peers inside.

Comet nods and then looks at Dawn. The two lock eyes for a second, and then the bard gives a huff and a serious expression to him. With a chuckle, Comet shrugs his shoulders and flips the watch around to face the group.

The girls, eager to figure out the watch's mystery, peer inside to see a blue screen with white dots and lines. The lines seem to form an exact map of Sol with the dots lining up with some of the cities that comprise it.

"This is the Hyperspace Timepiece." Comet smirks proudly. "And it is my magic item from my home world, the World of Wishes, Magnetar. It was given to me by our leader, the Zenith. It allows me to track the location of the Wishing Stars and will be our guide on our journey."

"Wait a second!" Zua looks up, excitement building up in her eyes.

"Do you mean?" Urania leans closer, a big smile painted on her face.

"We're going to find all the stars?" Dawn feels her heart begin to race.

"That's right!" Comet smiles from ear to ear. "You guys have proven these last couple of days that you are more than worthy and ready for this kind of mission. I need help, and I will reward you handsomely when we get all of the stars. What do you say? You want to go on the adventure of a lifetime with me?"

The girls look at each other rapidly. They weren't the best team, but they worked together well enough; being able to cover each other's weaknesses and build on the other's strengths. Plus, the notion of an adventure to track down wish-granting stars is not something that falls into your lap every day. They turn to face their hirer and humongous grins on their faces and let out a cry in unison.

"Yeah! Let's go!"

To be continued in *The Island of the Moon.*

ABOUT THE AUTHOR

Having grown up with a love for storytelling, YUMA knew at a young age that he was going to become an author. Though he struggled to make time for his work, with support from friends and family, he finally has been able to live his dream. His love and understanding for JRPG video games and cinema allows him to capture the fantastical worlds and stories that fill his mind on a daily basis. He wishes to entertain the world and make an impact on the world. Guess he is off to a good start.